"I don't even know what I am...."

"How could you do this to us?" Paul Fletcher's voice cracked. "We've done everything we could to be the best parents we could, for seventeen years, and now we get this!" He stood up and walked out of the room.

Molly, with tears streaming down her face, went to her mother and buried her head in her lap. "Mom, please — please understand. I love you so much. Please understand!"

Molly by Any Other Name

Jean Davies Okimoto

SCHOLASTIC INC.
New York Toronto London Auckland Sydney

"Da Ya Think I'm Sexy?" (Carmen Appice, Rod Stewart) © 1978 WB Music Corp., Nite Stalk Music, and Music For Unicef. All rights on behalf of Nite Stalk Music administered by WB Music Corp. and all rights on behalf of Music For Unicef on behalf of Rod Stewart administered by Intersong, USA Inc. All rights reserved. Used by permission.

An excerpt from *Roots* by Alex Haley, copyright © 1976 by Alex Haley. Reprinted by permission of Doubleday, a division of Bantam, Doubleday, Dell Publishing Group, Inc.

ISBN 0-590-42994-9

Copyright © 1990 by Jean Davies Okimoto.
All rights reserved. Published by Scholastic Inc.
POINT® is a registered trademark of Scholastic Inc.

12 11 10 9 8 7 6 5 4 3 2 1   6   3 4 5 6 7 8/9

Printed in the U.S.A.   01

For my brother, Roger Lewis Davies
a.k.a. Roger the Dodger
and
to Joseph Tsutomu Okimoto

In loving memory of my grandfather,
Lewis H. Williams

Acknowledgments

I would like to thank Donna Evans, former Executive Director of the Washington Adoptees Rights Movement and the other adoptees, birthmothers and adoptive parents who shared their stories with me: Carol Austin, Susan Mayrim Morgan, Sis Parlette and Barb Andrews. I also appreciate the help of Roger, Judith and Gwyneth Davies of Halifax, Nova Scotia, and of Tony Lee, son of Al and Lena Lee, of Vancouver, British Columbia. Steve, Dylan, Amy and Katie were wonderful resources, and I am grateful that my agent, Ruth Cohen, was persistent about my writing about this subject. I especially appreciate the editorial sensitivity and skill of Regina Griffin.

Molly by Any Other Name

Part One
Molly

One

"**M**olly Jane Fletcher! What's that all over your car?"

Molly leaned over the top of the VW bug, trying to figure out where the squeaky voice was coming from. No mistaking it. Mabel Wiley, of course, squawking about something or other. *Now* what was her problem? Molly wished that just once something would go unnoticed by Mrs. Wiley next door — or at the very least, that she wouldn't feel so compelled to answer Mrs. Wiley's every question.

"I said, 'WHAT'S THAT ALL OVER YOUR CAR, MOLLY JANE?' "

"It's toilet paper, Mrs. Wiley!" (It's none of your business, Mrs. Wiley.)

"What did you say, Molly Jane?"

"TOILET PAPER!" Molly yelled louder.

"Toilet paper, you say?"

"Yes, Mrs. Wiley. Toilet paper."

"Why did you put toilet paper all over your car?"

"I can't see you, Mrs. Wiley. Where are you?"

"Up here, dear, up here. I'm on the deck."

Molly put her hand to her forehead, shading her eyes, and peered up through the trees, finally locating Mrs. Wiley's white head poking through the upper branches of the Japanese maple. She was perched behind the tree on the second-story deck of her rambling gray house. Mabel Wiley's house was a bit in need of minor repairs; scores of rainy winters had wrinkled its face with peeling paint, and the spindly gutters were wobbly. But the structure itself remained sturdy, and the old house endured year after year, not unlike its owner.

Mrs. Wiley flailed her arms around. "Do you see me now, Molly Jane?"

Molly waved. "Yes, Mrs. Wiley. I see you." Opening the car door, Molly gathered her books and a large box from the front seat. Not today, definitely not today, Mrs. Wiley. Your babbling is the last thing I need right now.

She leaned over the front seat and leafed through her books trying to find the pamphlet. Which one had she hidden it in? French? No. Trig? Not there, either — she went through it twice, double checking. Where *did* she put it? She flipped through the pages of Our Heritage: The History of the United States. The last book — it'd better be here. Yes, finally — there it was, safely lodged between the Roaring Twenties and the Great Depression. The printing of the pamphlet jolted her again with its bold letters. NORTHWEST ADOPTEES SEARCH ORGANIZATION. As she stared at it, a toilet paper streamer floated into the car.

"Why did you put that toilet paper on your car, Molly Jane?" Mrs. Wiley yelled again.

Molly lifted her books and the box from the seat and slammed the door of the ancient car, which groaned and rattled in protest until it finally thudded shut. Leaning back against it, she wished she could shut up Mrs. Wiley as solidly. "I didn't put it there, Mrs. Wiley. Someone at school did."

"Why did they do that?"

Molly sighed. Would she ever have the nerve to go in the house without uttering a word to Mabel Wiley? Lately she noticed that she was getting quite tired of being nice — Molly Fletcher, such a *nice* girl. Barf.

"Molly Jane! Did you hear me? Why did they do that?"

"It's sort of to congratulate me, and it's a sign of affection, Mrs. Wiley. I just found out that — "

"It's a waste of toilet paper!"

Mabel Wiley then proceeded to lecture Molly from her perch on her deck on the subject of "waste." It was a standard Mrs. Wiley speech. Most of what she said began with "Young people today," which was followed by something bad, that would lead into, "now, in *my* day," which would be followed by something good, either about her job at Boeing during World War II when she was one of the original "Rosie the Riveters," or her years at the police department where she organized the first meter maid division. Either way, she always concluded that *she* knew something about real work, which today no one did.

As Mrs. Wiley finished a "Rosie" reference, Molly gave up the idea of explaining why her car had been t.p.'d in the first place. She started pulling the toilet paper off the car and stuffing it into an empty Safeway grocery sack. One side of the grocery sack was printed with information on missing children and on the other was the lettering *Keep Washington Green*. Everything here was green, but now gold had been added as fall had come early and quickly this September. The crisp, tart air had turned the leaves suddenly, while the north wind scattered their gold shapes across the lawns. Most people loved Seattle in the spring when the flowering apple, plum, and cherry trees and the rhododendrum blossoms as big as basketballs exploded with color. But Molly loved the fall; the apples were best, and the colors matched the bright green and gold colors of her school. Sometimes she felt sad it was already her senior year at Roosevelt. Things seemed to be moving too fast.

"Discipline. That's what it all comes down to — " squeaked Mrs. Wiley from the deck.

"I'm sure you're right about that, Mrs. Wiley. See you later."

Once in the house, Molly stood by the sink and looked out the window at Lake Washington. She wondered what to do with the pamphlet. Hide it somewhere? Stash it away like the sexy books she and Kathy had discovered when they were in the sixth grade? *Why did she feel so damn guilty?*

She walked slowly up the stairs to her bedroom and shut the door. It was a cozy corner room with sloping ceilings; her dad thought the nooks and crannies were made to order for a built-in bookcase and a window seat and had added them as soon as they moved in. Had she really been only six then? She crouched in front of the bookcase, staring at the shelf that held her childhood favorites — *Lyle, Lyle Crocodile*, *The Country Bunny*, *Curious George*, *Madeline to the Rescue*, *Why Was I Adopted?*

When had this last book first been read to her? All she could remember were the rainy days when they would have tea and cinnamon toast and, sitting close against her mother, sometimes nestled in her lap, she would listen and look at the pictures. Just another book like the one about the bunny or the monkey.

She got up, went over to her bed and opened the big box. Amazing. She had actually tried out for cheer squad, and without saying anything to Mom and Dad. Out of character, no question about it. Of course, when she mentioned it as a sophomore, her mother said it was — what were her words? Frivolous, yes, frivolous and exhibitionistic, that was it.

So of course, she hadn't tried out. Must always please Mom.

It seemed ludicrous to her, as she took the uniform out of the box, that in her family being a cheerleader could actually be construed as a rebellious act. But she did have to admit that since turning seventeen, she was finally getting more of a mind of her own. What had taken her so long? Ever since junior high most of her friends had been doing a lot of what they wanted — even if it didn't go over so well with their parents. Kathy quitting the youth symphony and joining the Roughriders All-Girl Band was a perfect example. Mrs. Barksdale had gone berserk, she had really lost it, but Kathy just did it anyway. And that was three years ago. Molly felt she had always been out of sync, late actually, with everything. Collecting stamps when her friends were first turning on to rock, a passion for horses while they went nuts over guys. Guys. When was that going to change? Would it ever? She got so anxious around them; clammed up every time a guy tried to talk to her. Except for Roland, of course. But he didn't really count — Roland was sort of like her brother, comfortable like an old shoe. She checked her watch — he should be here pretty soon.

Molly lifted the uniform out of the box, took off her jeans and blouse and slipped on the bright green sweater with the gold teddy bear patch and the letters *R. H. S.* It fit pretty well. She stepped into the green skirt, spun around flashing the gold inserts in each pleat then stopped and pulled at the hem. This skirt was seriously short. A person couldn't jump around with just underwear on under this thing — there must be some green trunks that go with it. She rifled through the tissue paper in the box. No trunks. All she found was the medical form required of all students who participated in sports; she was supposed to return it filled out before Friday. Funny, she never realized they put cheerleading in the sport category. Better ask them about the trunks when she returned the form.

At five-ten, Roland Hirada pulled up in front of the Fletchers' house in his deteriorating Chevrolet. Many years past its prime, it was an old clunker, a beater. Roland, who liked to name things, had christened it the M.M. — the Manure Mobile. But on the mornings it refused to start, which were frequent, he referred to the M.M. in more explicit terms.

Turning off the motor, he got out of the car and slammed the door. The radio antenna fell off. He got down on his hands and knees and groped for it as it rolled under the car toward the curb.

"Is that you, Ronald?" a voice squeaked from the yard next to the Fletchers'.

"Roland. My name is Roland, Mrs. Wiley," Roland yelled from under the car.

"What are you doing under your car, Ronald?" squeaked Mrs. Wiley, who was now raking leaves on her front lawn.

"It's Roland, and I'm looking for my antenna."

"What's it doing under your car?" Mrs. Wiley stopped raking.

"It fell off."

"Perhaps you should fix it, Ronald."

"Yes, Mrs. Wiley."

"Molly Jane is home," Mrs. Wiley announced.

"Yes, I know that. Good-bye, Mrs. Wiley." Roland stuck the antenna back on the car and trotted up to the front door and leaned on the bell.

As soon as she heard it, Molly ran down the stairs. Maybe I should have taken this thing off, she thought, feeling suddenly self-conscious as she opened the door.

Roland grinned as he stared at the uniform. "Nice. Very nice."

"Don't laugh."

"Who's laughing? You look great." He took off his jacket and threw it over the banister. "I knew you made it when I saw them t.p. your car."

"Want something to eat?" Molly asked as he followed her into the kitchen. "There's not much — they're both on diets."

"I'm not hungry. I made spaghetti for me and Justin. He was hungry so we ate early."

They went down to the family room in the basement. Roland flopped down on the couch while Molly turned on the TV and the VCR. Every day she taped *The Seasons of Our Lives*, her favorite soap.

"Are you supposed to cheer Friday night?"

"I think so." Molly sat down next to him. "I was

excited when I found out I made it. But now I'm just nervous — I'll look like a jerk — I don't even know the cheers."

"You'll do fine, don't worry about it."

"I don't even know why I tried out in the first place. It's certainly not the kind of intellectual pursuit my parents prefer."

"Who cares? Might as well get in all the rah rah crap we can."

"Yeah. I suppose that's why I did it."

Roland stretched out his legs and crossed his arms behind his head. "Do we always have to watch this?"

"I like it."

"Why do you tape this thing, anyway?"

"I don't know — maybe because it's consistent. You know, the same people struggling with problems year after year. There's something dependable about that."

"Scuzzy affairs, suicide attempts, murder — that's dependable? You have to be kidding."

"I am not. The same people show up, okay — their lives might be a mess, but you can always count on them being there Monday through Friday. Besides," she said, bristling, "a lot of people watch soaps. They always have 'em on in the dorms at the U."

"A lot of people are idiots."

"Are you calling me an idiot?" Molly punched his shoulder.

11

"If the foo shii — " Roland laughed.

"You are so dumb."

"Look — I only meant that just because a bunch of people, at the U or anywhere else, do something doesn't mean that thing is necessarily so great. And you don't have to hit me," he growled, grabbing her arm. "Don't mess with me, kid, I'm bigger than you."

"Most people are." She laughed.

"That's why I hang around you — 'cause you're a shrimp. Not even five feet."

"Gimme a break — " Molly yanked her arm away. "I'm five two. So how tall are you now, anyway?"

"Five nine, and I hope it's not over. Who knows? I might even have a shot at the pros. Atlanta has Spud — he's five eight, and the Bullets have the amazing Tyrone 'Muggsy' Bogues, who's five three. I could be the first Japanese-American in the NBA. Supposedly my dad still grew some in college."

"What I was trying to say about college kids is that the reason they watch soaps — "

"I was talking about basketball!" He slapped his knees, exasperated. "Here I tell you my secret dream — the first Asian guy in the NBA — I'd never tell anyone else this stuff — and you talk about soaps." He glared at her. "That's cold."

"Sorry. That's very nice if you could be in the NBA." She smiled sweetly. "Now I'll tell you why college kids watch soaps." Roland rolled his eyes as Molly continued. "The reason is that they're away from home where everything's strange so they turn to this familiar thing. Soaps — where they know all the people."

"This is probably more why they watch." He pointed to a gray-haired man and woman beginning to make love as the program broke for a commercial. "Everyone stays tuned in to see if they're gonna do it."

"Oh pul-lease." Molly shook her head.

"You know that lady and that man in bed — ?"

"What about them?"

"Do you ever think about people's parents doing it — you know, having sex?"

"What a weird question. I don't know if I ever really exactly thought about it, why?"

"I just can't imagine my parents having sex, that's all."

"I don't believe this conversation."

"The only evidence is us. Think about it, my parents had to have done it at least two times before they got divorced because there are two of us, Justin and I, and since you're an only child you know they did it at least once — 'cause you're here."

"No, Roland, I don't know that — remember I'm adopted."

"I forgot."

"Have you gone blind or something? How can you forget — in all the years you've been hanging around — I mean, we don't exactly match; I'm sure you must have noticed they're white and I look Asian."

13

"That's exactly the point."

"What is?"

"That I've been hanging around here all these years — since the sixth grade, to be exact."

"Has it been that long?"

"Yeah."

"Well, what's that got to do with it, anyway?"

"They're just your parents to me, that's all. I knew you were adopted, but you forget about stuff like that when you know people forever — whether they look like their parents or not. Anyway, I'm sorry." Roland yawned, and put his hand on her shoulder. "The soap's over. Let's watch ESPN."

"Okay." Molly switched off the VCR, and turned the TV dial, trying to find the sports channel for him. "Roland, do you have family psych?"

"I take it next semester, why?"

"We had this speaker today. She handed out some pamphlets and — "

"Molly!"

"What?"

"What are you wearing under that skirt?"

"It's none of your business, but underpants — why?"

"You mean you're going to be jumping around in front of the whole school in your underwear, and the guy yell leaders are going to throw you up in the air — I mean, the whole reason those guys are yell leaders is so they can grab the girls and throw them up in the air and look under their skirts."

14

"Don't be a jerk. There're some green trunks that go with it — everyone knows that — they just didn't put them in the box."

"I don't think I like this whole thing."

"I don't believe you sometimes. You say this weird stuff like you're my father or something."

Molly found ESPN and was sitting back down on the couch when she heard the garage door opening and the back door being unlocked.

"Dad's home."

Roland glanced at his watch. "Guess I'd better get going. Get those trunks, Molly. Just do it!"

"Oh, shut up. Come on." As she stood up, she grabbed his hand and pulled him up from the couch. "You weigh a ton!"

"It's all muscle. I could slam dunk you with one hand." He grabbed her around the waist, lifting her off the ground.

"Okay, okay. I'm impressed." She laughed, looking up at him.

As Molly walked Roland to the door they saw her father already settled in his chair in the living room, absorbed in the newspaper.

"Hi, Dad."

"Hello, Mr. Fletcher — I mean Dr. Fletcher." Roland had trouble remembering that Molly's parents were both doctors, her dad a Ph.D. and her mom a physician. He could never quite get it straight.

"Hi, kids," Dr. Fletcher mumbled and rattled the

paper, without noticing the green-and-gold uniform.

In the kitchen, Roland leaned back against the door. "You look pretty good in that thing."

"Thanks."

"Congratulations."

"Thanks."

"See you tomorrow. Don't forget the trunks for the Ingraham game."

"Get outta here." She smiled as she closed the door. At least Roland thought the cheerleader deal was neat. Dad hadn't even looked up from his paper.

Upstairs in her room, Molly put on some music. She went through the motions of a few of the cheers, looking at herself in the mirror in the uniform. Wish these stupid thighs weren't so big. Thunder thighs, that's what they are. Terrible. She yanked at the skirt, wanting it to be longer, then checked the box one more time for the trunks.

Molly flipped the record to the other side and flopped down on her bed. Lying there, she stared up at the canopy. Tiny white dots were woven into the soft sheer fabric. She used to imagine they were little stars, and would fall asleep counting them. Sometimes she made wishes on them, like they were real stars. She wished she had told Roland about the pamphlet. She had tried — she'd wanted to.

Molly closed her eyes. *Is it so wrong to want to know?* She felt a knot in her stomach. Sitting up, she reached for her books where she had left them on the end of the bed. She grabbed her history book,

16

found the pamphlet and slowly read the first paragraph.

The Northwest Adoptees Search Organization is a search and support group for adult adoptees, birthparents and adoptive parents. Adoptees under the age of 18 must have the permission of their adoptive parents in order for N.A.S.O. to act as their advocate in opening birth records, contacting birthparents and facilitating reunions with birthparents.

Molly's hands shook as she stuck the pamphlet back in the book. She got up and went to the full-length mirror attached to the back of the closet door.

Standing there, she studied her reflection, cataloging her features. Thick black hair . . . high cheekbones . . . dark Asian eyes . . .

She stared into her own dark eyes. *Who do I look like?*

Two

Molly opened her bedroom window and let the cool air drift in. She stood next to the window, fanning the sweater over her stomach. A person could roast in this thing — it better not get this hot at the game! She stayed by the window, her eyes scanning the street for a sign of her mother's car. Where was she? She should be home by now. This is crazy, she thought — can't believe I'm so uptight.

When she saw her mother turn onto N.E. Mills Street, Molly sighed and sat down on the window seat, watching the blue Volvo as it turned into the driveway.

Mom was so funny about that car. It absolutely irked her that Volvos were now considered the quintessential yuppie car. She reminded Molly that she had driven them since the beginning of time, certainly long before yuppies discovered them, and yuppies were definitely the last group Dr. Eleanor

Fletcher wanted to be associated with. "The self-involvement of these young upwardly mobile types and their lack of concern for anybody but themselves make them a very destructive generation," she'd declared. "Besides, at fifty-three I'm hardly a young professional — and I certainly don't want to be lumped with that bunch just because of the kind of car I drive!"

As the garage door rose, Molly saw Mabel Wiley rise up from behind the hedge. Her mother waved to her as she drove into the garage.

"Eleanor? May I have a word with you?" squeaked Mrs. Wiley.

Molly sat closer to the window. Can't anyone get in our house without talking to that woman? What a pain. Now what does she want?

In a few minutes her mother came out of the garage and walked over to the hedge. "How are you today, Mabel?"

"Oh, my back is acting up again but it's something that I have just learned to bear over the years — after all, someone has to rake all these leaves. And we all know that idle hands and an idle mind are the devil's workshop."

"Well, don't overdo it, Mabel."

"Thank you for your concern, dear. Now, Eleanor, there's something I feel I must speak with you about."

"Yes, Mabel, what is it?"

"It's about Molly Jane."

"Oh?"

Mabel Wiley leaned across the hedge. "She had toilet paper all over her car."

"Really?" Her mother sounded like she was trying to appear serious.

"Yes. Toilet paper."

"Thank you for telling me, Mabel."

"Well, I just thought you should know."

"I'll be sure and look into it, Mabel."

Molly yanked the window shut. Unbelieveable. Truly unbelieveable. Mom couldn't actually be serious about "looking into it." She was probably just humoring the old soul — that's what both her parents called Mrs. Wiley.

"Paul? I'm home — " Her mother's voice echoed through the house.

Jumping up from the window seat, Molly took off the uniform and carefully folded it over the footboard of her bed. Then, quickly, she leafed through her history book, checking to see if the pamphlet was still there. It's not going to disintegrate like something from *Mission: Impossible*, she reminded herself, staring at it for a minute before snapping the book shut.

She turned on the stereo and the room was filled with a hoarse wail. *If you want my body . . . And you think I'm sexy . . . Come on baby let me know*. The Rod Stewart concert two weeks ago had been great; she'd had her own revival of his early stuff in her room ever since. Molly grabbed her jeans and sweatshirt from the bottom of her closet and was changing into them when she thought she heard something. Listening a minute, she paused, then pulled the sweatshirt over her head. *Come on baby let me know.* Great song. Love that song. Her hips moved with the music, her voice merging with his rasping sound . . . *if you want my body . . . And you think —*

"Molly!" her mother called, knocking hard on the door.

Molly zipped up her jeans and ran to the door, yanking it open. The bedroom doorjamb was warped, and she always had to give it a good pull.

"Didn't you hear me?" Ellie ran a hand through her soft graying hair.

Molly shook her head, waiting to hear what her mother wanted.

There was a clumsy silence. Her mother seemed to just be standing there watching her. *If you want my body . . . And you think I'm sexy . . . Just reach out and touch me.* Ellie absentmindedly patted the brown age spots that were forming on the backs of her hands. "Turn the music down, honey. It bothers Dad," she finally said quietly.

"Okay." Molly walked to the stereo. She knew her dad wasn't the only one it bothered — and it wasn't just the volume, either. Her mother made no secret of the fact that she thought Molly's music was blatant and brazenly sexual, and she found that aspect of

21

it disturbing. Her idea of music was Benny Good-man, Glenn Miller, the big band sound; the music she'd loved when she was young.

Molly turned down the volume . . . *just reach out and touch me* . . . the husky voice was quieter now. Maybe now I could do it, she thought. Maybe now I could just sort of casually mention the pamphlet the lady handed out in class . . . like it was no big deal — just like how Mom read me that book *Why Was I Adopted?* — just like any other book.

"Mom?" Molly turned, but the door had closed.

She sat down on the bed. Why couldn't she just casually mention the pamphlet from the adoption place? Mom wouldn't drop dead. Maybe she could just leave it lying around — and then they'd see it — or maybe at dinner when Dad asked about how her day was, which he did religiously every night, she could say, "Oh, fine, we had a speaker in family psych from this organization for adopted people that finds their birthparents — pretty interesting, huh?" Then she'd just whip out the pamphlet, and Dad and Mom would say, "Oh, isn't that nice? Let's in-vestigate that."

This is getting ridiculous, she thought. She grabbed for the phone and punched in Roland's number. While it was ringing, she took the pamphlet out of her history book.

"Roland?"

"Hi. What's up?"

"I want to talk to you."

"Sure — right now?"

"Well, not on the phone. I want to be with you."

"You sound serious."

"It's just that I really have to talk to you and — "

"Can you tell me what it's about?"

"I can't — I mean not over the phone."

"Okay. Do you want me to come over?"

"No. We're having dinner soon — let's meet at the pizza place on 25th in about an hour."

She felt guilty the minute she hung up. Maybe she should call him back and tell him to forget it. Molly stared at the pamphlet. *All these adopted people want to find out — it can't be so wrong.* But she was still uneasy as she opened her notebook, unzipped the plastic pencil case and stuck the pamphlet inside.

Noticing the green-and-gold uniform folded over the footboard, Molly picked up the sweater, held it against her chest and looked in the mirror. Never thought this would be in the wardrobe. Incredible. They'd actually picked her. After a moment she folded the sweater and lay it in the box it had come in, taking out the medical form that had been included. She looked at it casually, the standard form that had to be signed by a physician — but the last section caught her eye.

23

4. Family history: Please indicate the health or cause of death of members of your family as best you can.

	AGE IF LIVING	AGE AT DEATH	INDICATE ANY SERIOUS DISEASES	CAUSE OF DEATH
Mother				
Father				
Brothers				
Sisters				
Children				
Spouse				
Others				

Indicate which of your relatives have had any of the following diseases:

Cancer _____
Heart trouble _____
Kidney disease _____
Strokes _____
Arthritis _____
Diabetes _____
High blood pressure _____
Mental or Emotional disease _____
Tuberculosis _____

24

Relatives? . . . I don't know anything. . . . *I don't know anything about who I am*. Don't I have a right to know these things?

Molly stuffed the form in her notebook and slammed it shut. Then she went to the mirror and practiced jumping, trying to jump higher and higher, jumping furiously, one jump after another.

"Molly!" Her father's voice boomed up the stairs.

Molly stuck her head out her bedroom door. "What?"

"What's going on up there? The ceiling's shaking!"

"I'm jumping — "

"Well, DON'T, and dinner's ready!" her dad hollered.

Exhausted, Molly shut off the stereo and went downstairs.

"You were doing what up there?" her father asked irritably.

"Jumping." Molly put a chicken breast on her plate.

"Why were you jumping?"

"Because I'm a cheerleader, and cheerleaders jump."

"Now, I'm confused," Ellie said. "I thought you decided your sophomore year that you didn't want to do that — be a cheerleader."

"I did — and that was two years ago." As they ate, Molly explained how they had a fall tryout to replace a cheerleader who had moved over the

25

summer. "I just decided to do it, that's all."

"I see."

"Just 'cause you think it's dumb doesn't mean *I* do — I mean, maybe I'm not like you, Mom."

"I never said it was dumb, Molly."

"No, you didn't. What you said was that it was frivolous and exhibitionistic; I remember it real well, Mom."

"I have my opinions, Molly, and you asked me what I thought — what am I supposed to do — lie?"

Molly put the half-eaten chicken breast on her plate and pushed her chair away from the table. "No, Mom. You should never lie." She grabbed her books from the kitchen counter. "I'm going out. I'll see you later."

"Just a minute, Molly. Where are you going?" Her father's voice was tense.

"I'm meeting Roland — he's going to help me study something for one of my classes."

"Molly, can't we talk?"

"Yeah, well, Mom, it would be nice if you had said something like congratulations — even if you had to fake it a little — or maybe wanted to see the uniform."

"Molly, you're not the only person in the world, you know." Paul Fletcher raised his voice. "Your mother happened to have had a very hard day, and I didn't hear you asking her about it. She spent her entire day in the Intensive Care Unit, and last night's admission — that baby that was beaten by the mother's boyfriend — died today."

Tears stung her eyes. "Yeah, Dad, well I'm sorry about that baby, but my whole life I've had to hear about Mom taking care of all the sick kids and all the dying babies, and I am just sick of it." Molly's voice caught in her throat. "Just once — just once I'd like her to be happy about something frivolous in this world and something fun that I do, like being a goddamn cheerleader!" She fled from the kitchen, slamming the door, knocking the rainbow magnets off the refrigerator onto the floor.

Molly climbed in her car and turned on the windshield wipers. It wasn't until she stopped at the end of the street that she realized it wasn't raining. Shutting off the windshield wipers, she fumbled in her purse for a Kleenex and wiped her eyes. She took a deep breath, put the car into gear, and turned left off Mills Street.

It was a clear night, a sprinkling of stars pierced the blue-black sky, and under the glare of the streetlight, brownish leaves dusted the sides of the road. The night air was chilly. Molly shuddered. Running out of the house she had worn only her sweatshirt. She pulled the cuffs down over her cold fingers and gripped the steering wheel. There was no use in turning on the heater in the old Bug. It took forever to warm up, and she'd be at the pizza place in a few minutes.

Heading down 25th, she turned in the parking lot and was relieved when she saw Roland's old beater parked in a corner. Roland was leaning back against the door, his hands in his pockets.

Molly turned in and parked next to his car. She pulled up the emergency brake and rolled down the window. "Hi, were you waiting long?"

He bent down and stuck his head in the window. "I'm freezing my butt off out here — let's go in."

"Okay — let me get my stuff." Molly grabbed her books and locked her car. As they walked up the steps into the restaurant, Roland put his arm around her narrow shoulders.

"Are you hungry?" He looked at the menu hanging over the counter.

"Yeah, I am — "

"I wasn't sure if you would be 'cause I thought you were going to eat with your parents — "

"I did, but I lost my appetite, but now I'm hungry again. Let's get a table and then decide."

They found a corner table on a lower level underneath a skylit window banked with ferns. The restaurant wasn't very crowded. Molly was glad the table was private and quiet. The last thing she wanted right now was to run into a bunch of their friends. She put her notebook on the table. "How much can you eat?"

"At least half a medium."

"We'd better get a large." Roland always ate twice as much as he said he would.

He got up to place the order. "And a large Coke?"

"Right."

While Roland was at the counter, Molly opened her history book. Taking out the pamphlet, she put it on the table, smoothing out its creases with the palm of her hand.

Slowly she opened it. Her eyes focused on the heading *BIRTHPARENTS* and then jumped to the paragraph below and its heading, *ADOPTIVE PARENTS*. She looked at one and then the other . . . *BIRTHPARENTS* . . . *ADOPTIVE PARENTS*. The lettering on the pamphlet blurred.

"Are you all right?"

Molly jumped. She hadn't heard Roland return. "Yes . . . I mean no — "

"What is it?" He put their Cokes on the table and sat down across from her.

She wiped her eyes and blew her nose.

"Did you have a fight with your parents or something?"

"Yes, but it's not really about that." She was quiet for a few minutes. "Roland, you know how we were talking about my being adopted this afternoon?"

"Sure."

"Well, today in family psychology this woman came from this organization, it's called the Northwest Adoptees Search Organization, and well — here — " She handed him the pamphlet. "She gave these out. It tells all about it. Would you read it? I have to go to the bathroom. I'll be back in a minute."

29

"Sure."

Molly slid to the edge of the seat and as she stood up, Roland reached for her hand. He held it for a moment.

"You're cold."

"I know."

"Here, put on my jacket." He stood up and wrapped his letter jacket around her shoulders.

"Thanks."

In the bathroom, Molly took a paper towel, wet it with cold water and held it to her eyes. She had a thought she couldn't remember having had in a long time. . . . Maybe she's right here in this pizza place now only I don't know it, and she doesn't know it. . . . Molly had thoughts like that before, but usually when she was in a big crowd of people at a Seahawks game in the Kingdome or like last summer when she wondered if her birthmother was in the crowd of 100,000 who lined the shores of Lake Washington for the Emerald Cup Hydroplane races. This is making me crazy, she thought, wadding up the towel and stuffing it in the waste can.

Molly walked quickly back to the table. Roland had picked up their order and was scarfing down the pizza. "Did you finish reading it? What do you think?" she asked anxiously.

"Does this mean that adopted people can find out who their real parents are now?"

"First of all, the lady said that the biological parents are called the birthparents — they use the word

30

birthmother because if you say 'real mother' it sounds like my mom isn't really my mom, and she is — but they call my parents the adoptive parents."

"So this means that when you're eighteen you can go to this thing and then they'll try and find your real — I mean your birthmother and then if they do, well — then what?"

"If she gives permission, they'll tell me who she is."

"Then what?"

Molly looked up at Roland. "Then we could meet."

"That's really heavy. Do you want to do it?"

"I never knew about anything like this until today. I'm kind of numb. For one thing, I can't imagine doing it without Mom and Dad with me, even when I turn eighteen and supposedly don't need their permission."

"Why not just wait and see what you want to do then?"

"I just can't forget about it — I'd like to at least know how I feel about it *now*." Molly turned her head away and looked out the window in silence. "I wish you'd understand," she mumbled after a few minutes.

"I'm trying. I don't know what you want me to say. I mean, I know this thing has gotten you upset, and I want to help — but I don't know what to do."

"You don't have to DO anything!" she snapped.

"Don't be mad."

"God — all I've been doing tonight is getting bitchy with the people I care about, first Mom and Dad and now you. I feel so screwed up." She turned and stared out the window again.

"Mol," Roland came around the table and sat next to her, "just talk to me."

"I was trying to — "

"I know, but try again. I'll shut up."

"I don't want you to shut up — I don't know why I'm so touchy about this."

"*Sure*, if you could find out who your birthmother is — it's casual — it's nothing."

Molly smiled, feeling less tense as she leaned against him.

"When did you first find out you were adopted, anyway?"

"It seems like I always knew," she said quietly, taking a slice of pizza. "Mom and Dad probably told me when I was so little that I don't remember. It's the kind of thing you just know — sort of like what sex you are, I suppose. Do you remember finding out you were a boy and not a girl?"

"No."

"It's probably like that for all that kind of stuff," Molly said thoughtfully, as she chewed the pizza. "Like when kids find out what color they are, like when did you find out you were Asian?"

"Seems like I always knew." Roland took a bite of pizza. "My grandfather — "

"Don't talk with your mouth full."

"You sound like my mother."

"Sorry, but I can't understand you with a mouth full of pizza."

Roland wiped his mouth and took a sip of Coke. "My gr-and-fa-ther," he continued, pointedly enunciating. "Better?"

"Better."

"Anyway — he was in the 442nd in World War II. He made a very big deal about telling me that it was made up entirely of guys of Japanese descent and the most highly decorated American combat unit. He used to show me all these medals he won. I really ate it up — I can't remember ever not knowing our family was Japanese. What about you?"

"I don't know *what* I am." Molly stared out the window and then turned to look at Roland.

"Did your parents ever tell you anything about your real — "

"Birthparents," she corrected. "Supposedly my birthmother was Asian. That's all I was ever told, and I suppose that's all my parents were ever told."

"So you could be Chinese, or Japanese, even?"

"Or Korean, or Filipino, or Vietnamese, or Cambodian, Laotian, or Thai — one time I looked at the map just to check out all the possibilities. Besides that — I was never told what the father was — who knows — I could be half one thing and half something else."

33

"It's obvious what you are — a whole Molly. ALL Molly."

"You are a good friend, you know that?" She felt tears welling up again.

"Thanks."

"I — I just remembered this funny thing." Molly smiled, dabbing her eyes with a Kleenex. "I used to play with a girl my age named Colleen Hauk when we lived in our old neighborhood. In first grade she went to a different school, and she wore this uniform, and she said it was because she was Catholic." Molly laughed and took another slice of pizza. "So I said that I went to the public school and wore regular clothes because I was adopted."

"Everyone knows there are two kinds of people in the world," Roland said, laughing with her.

"Yeah, Catholic and adopted."

"And you can tell them apart because the adopted people are the ones in regular clothes."

"That's very good, Roland."

"I know."

Molly chewed the pizza and became quiet, trying to remember when she had first wanted to know something about her birthmother. Probably around twelve, when Kathy Barksdale got her period before Molly got hers. She had wondered how old her birthmother had been when she had gotten her period — and what did she look like; was she tall, thin, short, stocky? What was her figure like? Did she have pimples? Molly was pretty sure that up until then she hadn't been very curious.

"You're so quiet."

"I was thinking about when I first began to wonder what she was like — and, well — why she didn't keep me. I remember this one time in the ninth grade, Kathy and I wanted to go to the midnight *Rocky Horror Picture Show* in the U district: Kathy's older sister said she'd pick us up, and we'd be home at three in the morning."

"Everyone does *Rocky Horror* at least once."

"Yeah. But Mom thought it was terrible to be out so late, and that we were going to throw rice and toast when they said 'toast' and dress up in bizarre stuff, and she wouldn't let me go."

"Did you want to run away or something?"

"No, but we had this big fight. I locked myself in my room, and that's when I thought that if I lived with my birthmother — I used to think of her as my other mother — that she'd let me go. She was this imaginary nice lady who let her kids go to the *Rocky Horror Picture Show* and throw toast."

"Did you want to meet her? Move in with her or something?"

"No. Never. I never thought it was possible to meet her. But more than that — I felt guilty about even the thoughts I had about her that time when I fought with Mom about the *Rocky Horror Picture Show*."

"Let's go and sit in my car." Roland looked at the

empty pizza box. "It's getting noisy in here."

In the car Roland turned on the radio, and Molly huddled next to him, pulling his green-and-gold letter jacket tight around her. They were quiet for a few minutes. Finally he asked, "Do you want to find her now?"

"I don't know. I'm so afraid to hurt Mom and Dad."

"So why not wait until you leave — after you graduate?"

"Leave home and then start a search for my birthparents? God, that seems cold. If I do it at all, I want Mom and Dad to be with me. But I'm afraid to tell them about this — " Molly pulled the pamphlet out of her pocket and stared at it. "I just wish I knew how they'd react."

"So why not go over to that place and just find out more about it?"

"Would you go with me?"

"Sure. I'll have to get someone to take care of Justin, but then I could go any day this week after school." Roland's hand brushed her cheek as he slipped his arm around her shoulder. His touch was warm, and Molly felt her face flush. Looking down, she fumbled with her notebook. "I have to go, Roland."

"Okay." He walked her to her car and waited while she got the engine started.

"Oh, I forgot your jacket."

"Keep it. You can give it to me tomorrow before third period."

When Molly got home only the porch light was on; her parents had gone to bed. The street was sheltered in fog as she parked the car and walked across the lawn toward the side of the house. Leaves crunched under her feet, and the grass was wet. She noticed that the Wiley house was dark and for that she was grateful. Mrs. Mabel Wiley often maintained her vigil by night as well as day. Molly reached the side door by the kitchen and fumbled in her purse for her key. Opening the door, she flipped on the light switch in the kitchen and was greeted by a sign taped to the refrigerator door.

It was the shape of a large megaphone cut from a grocery sack. It had a big letter R on it, written in black magic marker. A toilet paper streamer was attached to it and taped alongside it was a small note:

> *Congratulations, Molly!*
> *Love,*
> *Mom*

Three

Molly was standing in front of her locker, twirling the lock to her combination, when she felt a hand on her shoulder.

"Good morning." Roland's voice was cheery.

"Not so good — I've been asleep for most of it." She leaned against him and yawned. "Here's your jacket." She unlocked the locker and reached for his letter jacket.

"We didn't get home that late — "

"No, I'll tell you about it. Let's get out of here for lunch, okay?"

"Sure. I've got something for you."

"You do?"

"Sure do." He nodded. "I'll show you when we get to the car."

As they walked through the halls to the front door, Molly glanced up at the big banners that had been put up in preparation for the Ingraham game. The slogans, RAM THE RAMS and GO ROUGHRIDERS, were painted in huge letters and hung across the archways.

"Can't believe I'm actually going to get up in front of everyone and make a fool out of myself tomorrow night — I have no idea what I'm doing."

"Just jump around."

"Oh, sure."

"No one looks at the cheer squad that closely, anyway — people come to see the game. The cheerleaders are just decorations."

"They're what?"

"Decorations, cute decorations. That's why they have no ugly people on the cheer squad. You can't be so uptight about being a decoration — just chill out, Mol. All you have to do is look cute — that's easy for you."

"For some reason this conversation is not reassuring. In fact, I think it's a little insulting."

"Insulting? I was complimenting you. Didn't I say there were no ugly people on the cheer squad? It even says that in the bulletin when they announce tryouts: 'Ugly people need not apply.' "

"Oh, please."

"Didn't I say it was easy for you to look cute? That's a very charming thing to say."

"Guess I didn't catch that part. Your charm went right by me."

"Is that my fault? Pay better attention, and you'll start being charmed."

"Oh, honestly, Roland, saying I'll just be a decoration makes me feel like an airhead. Also I happen to know a lot of people who do look at the cheer squad. The problem is, I'm just not that spontaneous of a person — I've never done anything like this before."

"You seem nervous."

"That's what I've been TRYING to tell you!"

"Don't yell."

"I'm not yelling. Just listen to me. I'm starting to feel overwhelmed and don't come over tonight because I'm not going to be home. I'm going over to Kathy's — I want to talk to her before I call that adoption place."

He pushed the metal bar, opening the school's heavy front door. "When do you think you'll see Kathy?"

"Probably around eight."

"Tell her I want to talk to her, okay?"

"Sure."

They walked across the lawn and down 15th for two blocks to where Molly had parked her car. The sky was gray and overcast; a chilly wind rustled through the dry leaves, and Roland put his arm around her shoulder.

"Aren't you even curious?"

She nodded. "I want to see what it is."

"What what is?"

"What it is that you said you're going to give me — "

"I meant about why I want to talk to Kathy."

"I figured it's none of my business. If you wanted to tell me you would have."

He looked disappointed.

"Okay, why do you want to talk to Kathy?"

"I want to make a tape with her band and submit it to the MTV basement tape thing."

"That contest? Really?"

"You're not the only one doing something different this year."

"You know it's out of character for me to be on the cheer squad. Playing in a band isn't anything new for you."

"True. But I know I won't have time next year at the U, so it's now or never. Besides, Kathy's band is already organized — it makes it easier to sit in."

When they got to Molly's car, she unlocked the doors, and they climbed in. Roland had to move his seat back as far as it could go, trying to make the little car accommodate his legs.

"Do you want to drive anywhere?"

"No, let's just eat in the car and stay here. We don't have that much time."

Molly unwrapped her sandwich and took a bite. "Are you really serious about that tape thing with Kathy's band?"

"Sure. There's nothing to lose. I might even get famous and rich — I could quit working for 'tucky Chicken. 'Colonel,' I'd say, 'take this job and shove it!' " Roland laughed. "Then I could shoot baskets and hang out and also hire this lady who wears an apron to make my lunch." He bit into his sandwich. "I made bologna for Justin and me again today. He's on a bologna kick. You know, I think I've made our lunches my whole life. See, I'd hire this lady when I'm rich and famous, and she'll have this apron, and also she'd be there when I got home from my concert tours, and she'd have cookies in the oven. She would always be there — every day."

"Wanna bite?" Molly handed him her apple.

"Thanks. I like this green kind."

"Granny Smiths."

"They're good." He took a huge bite. "So what d'ya think of my idea?"

"You don't seem worried about making a fool of yourself — so that's good. Some people have big dreams and things, but I don't know how many ever try and do something about it."

"Me? Rockin' Roland Hirada make a fool of himself?"

"Well, you could, you know."

"Never!"

Molly glared at him. "Roland — I was NOT trying to put you down. Going for the MTV thing is great — no matter what happens. I wish I were more like that, that's all."

"You're perfect the way you are."

"I can't tell if you're kidding or not."

"Maybe I'm not."

"You know — I've always hated that word."

42

"What word?"

"Perfect."

"How come?"

"Because I always thought I had to be or else I might get sent back."

"That's sad," he said quietly. "Did your parents say that stuff to you?"

"No, nothing like that at all. I just thought it myself. But I'm telling you — this whole thing is really heavy. Last night when I got home, Mom had made a sign congratulating me about making the cheer squad — "

"That's great."

"I know, but I then had terrible dreams. I can't remember them, but I woke up at four-thirty all uptight."

"Well . . . here . . ." Roland reached in his pocket and took out a piece of carefully folded notebook paper. "In my first period class, African-American history, we're reading *Roots* by Alex Haley, and this is a quote from his book. I copied it down for you."

"This is what you meant when you said you had something for me?"

He nodded and handed the paper to her. "Sorry, my writing's not the greatest." Molly slowly unfolded the paper. The quote, written in his still-boyish scrawl, took up most of the page.

In all of us there is a hunger, marrow-deep,
to know our heritage. To know who we are

*and where we have come from. Without this
enriching knowledge, there is a hollow yearning. No matter what our attainments in life,
there is the most disquieting loneliness.*

"That's exactly it," Molly said softly to herself. She
read it over several times, tears welling up in her
eyes. After a moment, she held the paper to her
chest then folded it carefully and put it in her purse.
"Do you know that you are a very dear friend?" she
whispered.

Roland smiled. They looked at each other for a
moment, then he glanced at his watch. "We've got
to get back."

When they got to the corner across from the
school Roland stopped. "Look — it wasn't supposed to get you sad."

"It didn't. What it says is how I feel, that's all."

"Well, it's time to lighten up."

"I'm not sad, Roland, really."

"Okay. There were these two goats and they were
hangin' out in this field like goats usually do — "

"Oh, Roland — "

"Just listen. Now one of the goats finds this can
of film, and he eats it."

"Uh-huh."

"And his friend, the other goat, says to him, 'How
d'ya like the film?' "

Molly nodded attentively.

44

"And so this goat says, 'Well, I liked the film but the book was better.' "

"That was a *lot* better," she laughed, "than most of your jokes."

They stood at their lockers for a few minutes before the bell. "I guess I won't see you until tomorrow. I don't know how long the cheer squad practices — then I'm going to Kathy's."

"Don't forget to tell her to call me."

"Okay."

The bell rang, and Molly and Roland went down the hall in opposite directions. Halfway down the hall, she turned and ran back.

"Roland?"

As he turned around she gave him a hug. "Thanks." She held him close for a moment, but then saw how surprised he looked. "I — I'd better get to class," she stammered, and turned and headed quickly down the hall.

Four

Molly was alone in the locker room. The girls from the cross-country team had been there when she arrived, but had just left for their meet. She finished changing into her sweats and walked over to the mirror. Trying to seem energetic, she flashed her most enthusiastic smile, but it faded quickly.

This is stupid, she thought. Probably after practice they'll say they never should have picked Molly Fletcher. Molly looked around. The locker room suddenly seemed creepy. She didn't like being alone in there. Rhondelle Brown from the cross-country team had told Molly the football players crawled in the space above the ceiling from the men's locker room and made a hole in the wall of the women's shower. The janitor had patched it, but they still crawled around up there. Disgusting. What perverts! Better get out of here.

She glanced in the mirror one more time and trotted to the gym.

"Molly! Come on over!" Trish Barnes called.

Molly waved and ran to the corner of the gym.

"Joe and Chris aren't here yet," Trish said, "but while we're waiting for them, we'll teach you some stuff."

"I know most of the words, but I'm pitiful about the moves." She laughed nervously.

"You'll get it. Here — " Trish showed her. "It's easy. Just start with this — when we yell 'PUSH 'EM BACK' you move this way."

She copied Trish, picking up the moves quickly. They had time to go over four different cheers before Joe and Chris got there. When she saw them walk in from the men's locker room, Molly was surprised to realize she was feeling a little more confident.

"Molly, Joe's going to be your partner. You know everyone, don't you?"

She nodded. Chris was in her homeroom, and she knew Joe from her last year's chemistry class.

"We'll work on jumps — then if we have time we can work on the pyramid." Trish pointed to the pile of mats. "Grab the mats and spread out, everybody."

Molly glanced over at Joe as she walked with him to the middle of the floor. He had the muscular compact body of a gymnast — he'd been Metro champ in some event last season but she couldn't remember which one — maybe the rings or something. Since she was going to get thrown around,

47

she guessed it might as well be by him.

"You look a lot lighter than my old partner, Fletcher." He smiled. "This should be a snap."

"What happens if I start to fall?" she asked, not at all sure it would be such a snap.

"Remember the most important thing is trust. You've got to trust that I'll be right there." He dragged one of the mats to where she was standing.

"Okay." I hope the guy's at least half as strong as he looks, she thought. A crash landing is the last thing I need on this first little adventure.

"Okay. We'll do a few jumps first, and when we've got that together, you can practice standing on my shoulders."

"Okay," she gulped.

Joe put his hands on Molly's waist. "As you jump, I'll be lifting you."

"I think I'm afraid of heights all of a sudden."

"Don't worry. The best thing is to relax and forget I'm here. You'll be looser that way. Ready?"

"Yeah, here goes nothing."

Joe put his hands on Molly's waist again, and as she jumped he lifted her high in the air.

"Great! Okay, again — ready?"

"Yeah." Amazing. It wasn't that bad.

This time he lifted her higher, let go for a minute and then caught her coming down. "We're hot, Fletcher!"

"All right — I'm flyin'!"

It was exhilarating, going higher and higher.

48

There was something exciting about Joe. Molly remembered how he always had some girl hanging on him last year in chemistry. He had a reputation for being a big flirt. But she didn't think he was conceited — just very, very sure of himself. And in this situation, she decided, that was just fine. She sure wouldn't want to get thrown around by some nervous wimpy guy.

They had been practicing jumps for about fifteen minutes when Molly heard someone in the bleachers clapping. She looked up and the lone spectator waved vigorously.

Oh, no — what is *he* doing here? This is so embarrassing! Deciding to ignore Roland, she absolutely refused to look up there again, but it was difficult. He kept it up, clapping and waving at her for the next fifteen minutes. As soon as practice was over, she ran to the locker room, grabbed her stuff and headed for her car. She'd shower at home; she couldn't wait to get out of there.

As she turned the corner outside the gym, she bumped into Roland.

"Hi, you looked great!"

"Oh, Roland. How could you?"

"How could I what?"

"I was so embarrassed having you there clapping and waving like that — it was my first practice! I thought you had to take care of Justin."

"I do — I am. He's playing at his friend's house, and I have to pick him up in a few minutes. I came here because I thought you'd like my encouragement."

"You came to check up on me — didn't you?"

"Joe Abrams seemed to enjoy grabbing you like that." He scowled, looking down at her.

"This is ridiculous."

"Did you get the green underpants?"

"I refuse to discuss this with you — I've got to get home." Molly turned and stomped off.

"Are you still going to Kathy's?" Roland trotted after her.

"Yes," she said coldly.

"Well, call me when you get home."

"Oh, all right," she muttered, not looking back.

By the time Molly got home she had stopped being quite so mad at Roland. Who can figure the guy out? she thought as she parked her car in front of her house. He does something wonderful like giving me that *Roots* quote, then he turns around and acts like a jerk.

Mabel Wiley was in the front yard, weeding in the flowerbeds. Molly walked to the house as quickly as she could.

"Hello, Molly Jane." Mrs. Wiley bent over the beds, not bothering to look up.

"Hello, Mrs. Wiley."

"You know it's very important to get all the weeds out before the bulbs go in. Weeds grow in the fall, too, but a lot of folks forget that, Molly Jane."

"Yes, Mrs. Wiley."

"Your mother is home, Molly Jane. But your father hasn't arrived yet."

"Thank you, Mrs. Wiley."

"Don't mention it," she said, pitching a weed over her shoulder.

"Molly? Is that you?" Ellie called from the living room where she was reading the paper. "Did you stay late after school?"

"Hi, Mom." Molly stuck her head in the living room. She hadn't seen her mother since their fight the night before. "We had cheer squad practice — how was your day?" she asked uneasily.

"Fine." She put the paper down, her eyes anxiously meeting her daughter's. "How was your day?"

Molly walked over and sat on the arm of the couch. "Thanks for the note last night, Mom. I'm sorry I — "

"I'm sorry, too, Molly. Dad and I are interested in the things that are important to you — we want to go to one of the football games when you cheer."

"Well, you won't have long to wait. I'll be out there in front of everyone making a fool of myself Friday night at the Ingraham game."

"I'm sure you'll do fine. Would you like Dad and me to come?"

"It might be embarrassing — " She hesitated, then smiled. "But, yeah — I would." Molly gathered up her books and headed toward the stairs to go up to her room. "You didn't tell me much about your day, Mom."

Ellie folded the newspaper. "Better, much better than yesterday." As she walked toward the kitchen, she touched her hand to Molly's cheek. "We'll eat about seven — are you planning to be around here tonight?"

"I'm going over to Kathy's after dinner."

"Oh, well, tell her mother 'hello' for me if you see her."

Molly was uneasy as she closed the door to her room. Maybe she should forget going to Kathy's — just forget the whole thing. She ran a hand through her hair. Why does everything have to be so complicated?

She turned on the shower, then opened her purse to read the quote from *Roots* again when the phone rang.

"Hi, Molly." Roland's voice was friendly.

"Hi."

"Are you still mad?"

"No, but Roland — I just think we have a very bizarre relationship."

"No, we don't. Listen, I've made a great decision about how I can be part of the cheer squad," he announced. "I'm going out for the bear."

Molly was silent.

"You know, the teddy bear — the mascot. I'm going to try out for teddy bear."

"They already have a bear," she said disgustedly. "You know, I really don't need you to be in this with me."

"I thought it would calm your nerves to know I was by your side right there inside the bear uniform."

"It's a costume."

"Okay, so I'd be inside the bear costume."

"Listen, Roland. I've gotta go. I'll call you when I get back from Kathy's."

Molly felt like she was betraying her parents the minute she left the house. When she pulled up in front of Kathy's house she sat in her car, afraid to go in. What will Kathy say? Molly wondered, as she stared at the Barksdales' immaculate lawn. She loves my parents. Maybe she'll think I'm ungrateful to them — that I'm awful. She took a deep breath. Well, I won't find out sitting here, she thought, finally opening the car door.

"Come on up to my room," Kathy chirped, happy to see Molly. "I'm the only one home; my folks are at the symphony. Do you want anything to eat?"

"No, thanks — I had dinner before I left." Molly followed her up the large circular staircase and stared at Kathy's hair. Incredible. It was even a little more extreme than it had been the week before. Part of it was long and part was cut to only a quarter of an inch like an army haircut. That was one of the things she liked about Kathy: She never gave a damn what anybody thought.

"How do you like my hair?"

"What hair?"

"Don't tell me you didn't notice!"

"Just giving you a hard time." Molly laughed. "It'll be great for the band."

"My mom and I fight about it every day. She hates my hair, she says she's ashamed to be seen with me."

"That's really too bad."

"She's convinced I'm a druggie."

"You're kidding."

"I'm not — just 'cause my hair is not the way she wants it, she thinks my life is going down the toilet. Like tonight — they went to the symphony, you'd think they could just leave, go to the symphony and have a nice time — but instead, we have this big fight. They start lecturing me on their way out the door on good music and telling me to quit the band and go back to playing the violin in the Youth Symphony. And now she thinks I'm doing drugs because of my hair." Kathy went over to her stereo. "What d'ya wanna hear?"

"Anything."

"A little Stones, for old times' sake?"

"Sure." Molly sat on the floor, took off her shoes and looked through Kathy's albums.

"Do you know Susie Hildebrandt?" Kathy took the album out of its cover."

"In the band?"

"Yeah, she plays drums. She has an earring in her nose, and her parents didn't say a word."

"Oh, speaking of the band, Roland wanted me to tell you that he wants to talk to you. I think he's going to call."

"What about?"

"I'm not sure exactly. He has some idea he wants to talk to you about for one of those MTV basement tapes."

"He's so great, Molly. I mean, not just 'cause he's so good-looking."

"Roland?"

"Of course, Roland. Who d'ya think I meant?"

"Oh, yeah, Roland — "

"He's in my geometry class — sits between me and Megan Lee. That girl is all over him."

"You're kidding."

"No way. She's always asking him to help her with her geometry, and she wiggles all around him, just sticking her sexy little body right into him."

"You know, I never liked her."

"Well, the guys sure do. The other day I heard her telling Roland she thought he was the funniest guy she ever met — he just ate it up."

"He did?"

"Certainly did. Then she said she just couldn't wait until basketball season started, and he practically drooled."

"I didn't think he was that stupid."

"What's with you two, anyway? You sure are together a lot more than ever. Someone asked me the other day if you were going together."

"Me and Roland? That's ridiculous — we're just friends. Roland's like a brother to me. Who asked you, anyway?"

"I can't remember — let's see, it was a guy. Oh, yeah. It was Joe Abrams."

"He's my partner on the cheer squad."

"Now, *that's* another guy who's fine-looking."

"I know. But there's something about him that's just a little too cool — you know what I mean?"

"Kind of. Is that what you needed to talk to me about? It wouldn't surprise me at all if Joe started coming on to you. You're new — a challenge."

"No, it has nothing to do with guys. It's about my parents."

Kathy looked worried. "Is everything okay with them?"

"Oh, sure — they're fine. I'm just not sure I am." Molly stared down at the floor. She began picking little pieces of fuzz off the carpet. "I don't know where to begin. . . ." Her voice trailed off. She was quiet for a moment, unaware that she was still picking at the carpet. Finally she looked at Kathy who was sprawled across the bed. "Kathy, yesterday in family psych we had a speaker from an organization called the Northwest Adoptees Search Organization — they handed out this pamphlet." Molly took the brochure from her purse and gave it to Kathy.

She watched her friend closely as she read it.

When Kathy had finished, she turned the volume down on the stereo and handed the pamphlet back to Molly. "Wow. That's really heavy."

"That's exactly what Roland said."

"Do you want to do it?"

"I don't know how Mom and Dad would take it. You know them so well — what do you think?"

"Gee, Molly. I just don't know. I mean, I can see doing it someday — but why now?"

"I'm not sure, but I know I've wondered who my birthmother was for a long time, except that finding out seemed unthinkable."

"That finding out would be impossible? Or wrong somehow?"

"Both — it seemed wrong, and also I *never* thought it was possible. Kathy, you just can't imagine what it was like to hear that woman in class. There are all these other people that are adopted who want to know, too! It was incredible. It's as if I've suddenly been given permission."

Kathy rolled over on her back and folded her hands behind her head. Her hair stuck out in all directions. "I would want to know, too," she said quietly.

"Then you understand?"

"I think so." She sat up. "This isn't because you're mad at your parents or anything like that? If I were adopted, and I brought this up, my parents would think it was because of all the fights we've been having."

"No, the last thing I want to do is hurt Mom and Dad — that's what I'm so worried about."

"I wouldn't worry, then. Your parents are pretty understanding — pick a right, any right, and they've been for it. Human rights, civil rights, women's rights, gay rights — ever since I've known them they've been for all that stuff. Seems to me that since this is another one of those rights, they'd be for it. Here, lemme see that again."

Molly handed the pamphlet back to her, and Kathy scanned it quickly. "See, it says here" — she read from the pamphlet — " 'the right of an adopted person to know their heritage.' "

"I'm sick of not knowing what I am. It's crazy. All I know is I'm supposed to be Asian. That's all — I don't know if I'm Chinese or Japanese or Korean — or what."

"We've never talked about this" — Kathy went to the stereo and flipped the record — "but, does it bother you being Asian? Like in this day and age are you treated any differently than I am? Is anything different for you than it is for me?"

"Sometimes I've wished I was white like my parents, but I guess that's just so it wouldn't be so obvious to everyone that I'm adopted." Molly was quiet, thinking about it for a minute before she continued. "Seattle has a lot of Asians, and I guess it's a pretty open place to grow up. Also, with my parents being who they are with the kind of friends they have, and me going to Roosevelt, which is so

58

mixed — I can't say that I've ever felt any kind of racism."

"So there aren't any differences?"

"No, not entirely. There have been things that a white person wouldn't encounter. Like just a few months ago, I was at Zieter Shoes, and the clerk asked me if I spoke English. That's something that would never happen to you."

"Were you offended?"

"I just thought he was an idiot. Sometimes you just run into people like that who make assumptions because of color. No one's color-blind."

"Yeah, I know."

"There have been times, too, when I've been in eastern Washington with Mom and Dad, and there's a definite feeling of being different, a kind of conspicuous feeling you have because in some of those small towns it's pretty red-necked. Don't get me wrong, no one has ever treated me badly, but it's just a very different feeling, an awareness that my color is different from the majority. It's not a feeling I have in Seattle very often — but it's a feeling I wouldn't have if I were white."

"You know, it seems to me your parents would be the last people not to understand that you want to find out about this stuff."

"Then you think I should go ahead?"

"Molly, you're the only person who can decide. I just think your parents are pretty understanding, that's all."

It was raining when Molly left Kathy's house. She turned up her coat collar and ran to the car. As she was unlocking the car door, she glanced up at the light in Kathy's bedroom window. She was glad she had come over to talk to her. It had really helped. Kathy was right; her parents were understanding, and she was pretty sure that emphasizing wanting to know her heritage would be less threatening to them than focusing only on wanting to meet the actual person, her actual birthmother. Sometimes that idea was even too much for her to comprehend.

At home, she got ready for bed before calling Roland. "Hi, it's me. I'm back." She turned off the light and pulled the phone next to her, snuggling down under the covers. "Roland? I didn't wake you up, did I?"

"No, I'm trying to talk quietly. Justin fell asleep in my room, and I haven't carried him to his bed yet. I just talked to Kathy."

"You must have called her right after I left."

"I did. She thinks my idea's fresh — she's going to talk to the rest of the band about it tomorrow."

"That's great. Hey, what's this about you and Megan Lee?" she teased.

"What?"

"I thought you had better taste than that."

"She's not a sleaze queen. Anyway, what about you and that Joe Abrams? You know why all the girls call him Prince Charming?"

"Why?"

"Because every time they kiss him, he turns into a horny toad."

"That is so dumb. That is the dumbest of all your dumb jokes."

"No courtesy laugh?"

"Honestly, it's ridiculous. I hardly know him."

"Well, I hardly know her."

"I thought you'd be able to see right through her, Roland."

"She's actually a very nice person."

"Oh, sure. If you like Barbie dolls."

"Barbie dolls are blonde — Megan's Chinese."

"It doesn't matter, it's a type that's all."

"Are you going to tell me how it went at Kathy's or aren't you?"

"Sure. Kathy was great. I didn't say anything new over there — but it really helped to talk to her. She thinks my parents can handle it."

"That's good."

"Roland?"

"What?"

"I decided to do it."

"You mean go through a search and everything?"

"No, I'm still not sure about that. But I definitely want to call that place tomorrow and make an appointment to find out more about it. I'm going to call them at lunch. Will you stay and wait for me while I call?"

"Okay, if you want me to."

"I do."

Molly slept better that night. The next day during her lunch period, Roland walked with her to the pay phone outside the main office. She fumbled in her purse until she found a quarter, then dropped it as she went to open the door of the phone booth.

"Pretty nervous, huh?" Roland picked up the quarter and handed it to her.

She nodded. "It's all I could think about this morning. Last night it seemed so clear, but today I got all uptight again. I thought maybe I should just forget calling and forget the whole thing."

"You can, you know."

"I know I can. But something won't let me. Right now anyway, I feel like I have to do it." Molly opened the door of the phone booth. "Roland?"

"Yeah?"

"Stay here."

"Sure."

"I mean, don't go away — wait for me, okay?"

"Sure. I'll be right here."

Molly's hand shook while she deposited the quarter. It kept shaking as she took the pamphlet from her purse, read over the phone number and punched the buttons. The phone was answered after only a few rings, but it seemed to her like it took forever.

"Good afternoon. This is N.A.S.O."

"Hello — uh — my name is Molly Jane Fletcher." Molly's voice cracked and she cleared her throat. "And I was wondering if I could come in and talk to someone there about — about your organization."

"I'm Mrs. Sadock, the director of N.A.S.O., and I'd be glad to talk with you." She paused, then asked matter-of-factly, "Is this about a search?"

"Well, not exactly — I mean, I don't know. I'm an adoptee, and well, I guess there might be the possibility of doing a search, but right now I just would like to find out what all is involved."

"When would you like to come?"

"Would you be able to see me early next week?"

"Hold on a moment while I look." Molly started reading the graffiti that had been carved in the phone booth. After a minute the woman came back on the line. "Hello, yes, we do have some time Monday afternoon. We could see you at four."

"That'll be fine."

"Good, Monday at four. What was the name again?"

"Fletcher. It's Molly Jane Fletcher."

Molly stood in the phone booth for a moment still holding the receiver even though the line had gone dead.

She closed her eyes. Dear God, she thought, please let me be doing the right thing.

Five

"GO ROUGHRIDERS!!" Joe's voice boomed over the track while he held Molly above his head silhouetted against the blue-black sky. The scoreboard lit up the north end of the field: Roosevelt 0, Ingraham 7; while under the stadium floodlights the Roosevelt fans sat huddled together in their winter parkas, stomping their feet on the bleachers, trying as much to warm their feet as spur on the team.

"Brrrr. It's freezing!" Molly's voice was raspy from yelling. "Can't believe it's only September. I'm not so sure about this job!" She clapped her hands together.

"Just keep moving. You're so light, Fletcher, I could throw you around all day. Once more, ready?"

"Okay."

"GO ROUGHRIDERS!!" Joe's deep voice roared out over the crowd; Molly's croaked. Throwing her high in the air, he caught her easily then guided her back to the ground. "You're not going to have a voice left, and it's still the first half," he said, keeping his hands on her waist.

"I know, I sound ridiculous."

"Sounds sexy to me, Fletcher." His voice was low as he leaned down, brushing his face against her cheek.

"Sure, if you like bullfrogs." She turned toward the field to watch the game.

Ingraham had the ball on the Roosevelt thirty-yard line just a few yards from where she stood. Molly had never seen football from anywhere but up in the stands before, at least not for more than a minute. Hearing the grunts, the growled obscenities and the crack of helmets, made the players and the game in front of her loom large and dangerous. From up above it had seemed merely rough.

Out of the corner of her eye on the track, she saw Joe put his arm around Trish Barnes, then pick her up and spin her around. Molly tried to focus on the game, but she couldn't help watching Joe and Trish. Trish seemed to eat it up — what was with that guy? He sure liked to handle all the girls, and what really floored her was that no one seemed to mind. Even Trish, and she was no dummy.

It must be that the guy's so gorgeous no one can ignore him. Well, I'm going to, she thought, determined to keep her eyes focused on the field.

"PUSH 'EM BACK! PUSH 'EM BACK! — WAY

BACK!" As the squad yelled, Joe ran over to Molly, grabbed her hand and pulled her to the end of the line they were forming. "Get with the program, Fletcher."

"Okay . . . okay . . . PUSH 'EM BACK! PUSH 'EM BACK," she croaked, extending her right arm and resting it on Joe's shoulder, pumping her left arm with the others like a locomotive, trying to remember to jump back each time they yelled, "WAY BACK!"

"All right! That's it!" Joe bellowed as the line broke up.

"That's what?" Molly looked puzzled.

"The half. We held 'em!"

"Oh, yeah."

"Don't you know anything about football, Fletcher?"

"Of course I do."

"I think you need a lesson from me."

"I think I know all I need to know."

Slipping his arm around her shoulder, Joe rested his hand on the back on her neck. "I'd enjoy teaching you, Fletcher."

"Oh, sure."

"Why don't I give you a ride home after the game."

Molly tried to answer him, but the band gave a long drumroll, and the loudspeaker blared, blocking out all the sound on the field. "LADIES AND GENTLEMEN . . . TONIGHT . . . THE ROOSEVELT ROUGHRIDERS ARE PROUD TO ANNOUNCE THE

DEBUT OF OUR OWN ROCKIN' ROLAND HIRADA
. . . PLAYING FOR THE FIRST TIME TONIGHT WITH
OUR FAMOUS ROUGHRIDERS ALL-GIRL BAND!
LET'S GIVE 'EM A GREAT BIG HAND!"

"I didn't know they were playing at the half." Joe
stood behind Molly with his hands on her shoulders.
The yell leaders lined up along the fence, cheering
as Roland and the band members ran out on the
field.

"I didn't know, either. I guess they meant to surprise everyone." She jumped up and down, waving
to Roland and Kathy in the band. "This is weird —
I feel like a groupie or something!"

The crowd roared its approval as Roland picked
up his guitar and the Roughriders All-Girl Band
struck the first cord. Contrasted with the high voices
of the girls singing backup, Roland's voice wailed
rich and deep.

"The guy's not bad." Joe glanced back at the
stands where everyone was cheering.

"He's great!" Molly's cheeks were flushed. "Roland never said a word to me about doing this. Kathy
didn't, either." She looked up in the stands, where
the Roosevelt crowd was clapping with the beat.
"They really love them!"

The band finished just as the team came back out
on the field, and Roland ran across the track toward
the parking lot.

"Roland! Where are you going?" Molly ran after
him.

"Hi. What d'ya think?"

"You guys were great. You never said a word — "

"No, we decided to surprise everyone. Guess it went over okay, huh?"

"It definitely did. Listen, can I get a ride home with you after the game?"

"I gotta get my guitar home. I'm afraid to leave it in the car — might get ripped off. Why don't I meet you at your house, then we can go get something to eat? Can you get a ride okay?"

"Sure, I'll just go home with my parents."

"Oh, yeah, I forgot they were here."

"I waved to them earlier; they're up on top over on the left where the parents always sit. I guess I'd better run up and tell them I'll meet them at the car."

"It's such a mess after the game, you'd probably never find them in this crowd." He looked toward the parking lot. "Well, I gotta get going." Roland turned and headed toward the gate, then stopped and looked back. "Molly?"

"Huh?"

"Uh — was it really okay?"

Molly smiled. "Yes."

"Really?"

"You were wonderful."

The final score — Roosevelt 17, Ingraham 7 — was a smashing victory for Roosevelt. Going into the game, Ingraham ranked number one in Metro and had been expected to win easily. The upset was met with mayhem; the Roosevelt fans began pouring onto the field while the band played "Louie, Louie." The stands shook as the people in the bleachers stomped up and down, while down on the track, the cheerleaders stood hugging each other. Joe grabbed Molly and pulled her against him, then held her as a group of guys who had been getting high under the stands crawled out and staggered around the two of them.

"Come on, Fletcher, I'll show you where my car is."

"I've got a ride with some people — thanks."

"Tell 'em you're coming with me."

"I can't — I've got plans. See you later, Joe." Molly broke free and ran off into the crowd toward the parking lot. She had been moving around so much during the last half that she had forgotten about the cold, but now as she wound her way through the fans heading out of the stadium she began to feel it. She hoped the car wasn't too far — it was freezing. Pulling the sleeves of her sweater down around her hands, she scanned the lot, finally seeing her parents waving to her from the north corner. She couldn't believe she had told Joe she was going home with some people. Why hadn't she told him the truth? What did she care if he thought she was a nerd?

When Molly got to the car, her mother rolled down the window, motioning to her. "Come on — we've had the motor running, and the heater is just starting to warm up. You look frozen!"

"I am — it feels more like January or something. Can't believe how cold it got."

As she was getting in the car Joe walked by with a group of senior guys and caught her arm, glancing at her parents in the car. "So you're that scared of me, Fletcher?"

She stared at him, not knowing what to say. Then she mumbled, "I have to go."

"I'll call you." He said softly, letting go of her arm and disappearing into the crowd.

Slamming the door, she slunk down in the backseat, feeling like a complete fool. Of all people, wouldn't you know he had to show up.

"You must be tired, honey." Ellie looked back at Molly as her father headed the car out of the lot.

"Yeah, I am kind of. How'd you like the game?" she asked, trying to forget about Joe — that jerk.

"It was a lot of fun. Sure was cold, but you looked great down there in front doing those cheers."

"How'd you like it, Dad?"

"Good game. Good game."

"Are you really glad you went?" She wondered if they were just being polite.

"I'd love to go to another one. But next time I'll make a thermos of coffee."

"Make two, one for each of us," her father added as he turned onto Mercer Street.

"And the cheerleading — it's a great way to let

70

off steam, isn't it? Jumping around and shouting like that."

Molly looked out the window at the cars loaded with kids; the Roosevelt cars had piles of people hanging out the windows, honking and waving at everyone. Good old Mom — she's trying to be a sport about it, really trying to find something nice to say. If you can't find something good to say, don't say anything at all. How many times had she heard that growing up?

"It was fun to watch you. I thought my daughter was the prettiest girl out there — " Her dad stopped at a red light. "That boy who was throwing you around certainly seemed to think so, I'd say. Who is he?"

"Joe Abrams."

"We don't know him, do we? Has he been over to the house?"

"No."

"Well, I'd watch him if I were you."

"Oh, Daddy." Molly looked out the window. This is so stupid, she thought. Now I wish I *had* ridden home with him.

"Paul. Molly knows what she's doing." Ellie patted his arm. "Speaking of young men, Roland was sure a surprise at the half. I thought he was terrific."

"He sounded constipated to me," her father muttered.

"That's the style, dear. What's his name, Springsteen; sounds just like Roland."

"He'll like that, Mom. I'll tell him. He's coming over as soon as we get home."

The traffic had thinned out once they got away from Seattle Center and the stadium. Except for Molly's asking her mother to turn on the radio, they rode along the freeway the rest of the way in silence. As Paul turned into the exit lane near the university, he tried to catch Molly's eye in the rearview mirror.

"Molly?"

"Yeah, Dad."

"There's a new family at the lab."

"Oh."

"New baby pigs — "

"Uh-huh."

"Little tiny ones."

"Oh. That's nice." Molly looked out the window. Why was it, she wondered, that whenever he tried to connect with her, he'd say something about the pigs? She had named all the baby pigs they used for research at his lab when she was little, but it had been years since she'd been down there with him. Didn't he know how else to talk to her?

Molly changed into her jeans and was watching TV, waiting for Roland in the family room. Sometimes the eleven o'clock news showed a little bit of the high school games, and she was hoping the Roosevelt-Ingraham game might be on. Whenever she watched TV, she switched off the commercials — but when the next one appeared, she listened appreciatively. She had seen it dozens of times; a public service commercial about adoption, showing famous adopted people like former President Gerald Ford and Greg Louganis, the Olympic diver. Sometimes deep down, being adopted made her feel like a "throwaway" person, someone unwanted and not worth much, but whenever she saw that commercial she felt more valuable.

When she heard Roland drive up, she flew upstairs to let him in, trying to get there before he rang the bell and woke her parents.

"Hi, are you ready to go?" Roland stood on the porch dancing around like a boxer. "Man — I'm freezing my butt off out here."

"Well, come on in."

"Aren't you ready to leave? I thought we were going to get something to eat." He entered the kitchen as Molly closed the door behind him.

"Where do you want to go?"

"A bunch of people are going to Burger King on 35th — then there's supposed to be a keg at the Laurelhurst playfield."

"I don't know — let's just order pizza or something. If we go to Burger King we'll get all this pressure to go to the playfield, and the last thing I feel like doing is standing around in the cold again. Besides, I hate those things — people just get drunk and throw up."

"I never do that."

"I didn't say you did — I just don't like the whole scene, that's all."

"Fine by me. By the way, speaking of standing around in the cold, you looked pretty good out there tonight."

"Thanks."

"The H.T. sure enjoyed grabbing you."

"The H.T.?"

"Joe Abrams, the horny toad."

"Oh, Roland. Chill out." Molly got the phone book and opened it, riffling through the pages. "How much can you eat?"

"A large — easy."

"Okay. Coke?"

"No. I've got a couple of beers out in the car. I'll go get 'em since we're staying here."

"Okay." Molly ordered the pizza while Roland went back out to the car. When he returned he followed her to the family room and turned on the TV, dimly lighting the room with its fluorescent glow.

"There's nothing on. We should've rented a movie," he said, flipping around all the stations.

"The video place is closed — just watch MTV. You always like it."

Roland flopped down on the couch next to her and opened his beer. "Don't you wonder about some of those groups" — he took a drink and gestured toward the TV with the can — "like if they used to be some crummy garage band in high school."

"Probably most of them did — people have to start somewhere."

"The odds are totally against it. I bet the percentage of people who make it in rock out of all the zillions of people who want it is minute — almost zero."

"Sure, but that shouldn't stop a person from trying. You were really good tonight."

"No autographs, sorry."

Molly laughed. "I couldn't believe it. I felt like some stupid groupie — it was weird I got so excited when I saw you out there."

"What's weird? Why shouldn't old Rockin' Roland excite women? Why shouldn't he have a groupie? You look like great groupie material to me."

"Oh, Roland."

"And for your information, I am seriously writing some original material for the basement tape contest."

"Really? Do you have anything finished?"

"I have the first few lines of a song — it's awesome. Move over, Boss."

"Oh," Molly laughed, "I should tell you Mom said you sounded like him. They were so nice tonight. I'm sure Mom still thinks being on the cheer squad is stupid, but they're both really trying."

"How'd your dad like it?"

"He was sweet; he said I was the prettiest girl out there."

"I meant, how'd he like me?"

"He said you sounded constipated — " Molly was interrupted by the phone ringing. "I'd better get that. I'll be right back."

She ran up the stairs to the kitchen, flipped on the light and grabbed the phone.

"Hello?"

"Molly?"

"Yeah?"

"It's Joe. A bunch of us are at Trish Barnes's house. We're all going over to the playfield at Laurelhurst — they've got a keg. I'm coming over to get you."

"No, really. I can't — "

"I'm coming over."

"Joe, I'm with someone."

"Sure, just like you were going to ride home with some people. You don't have to be so damned scared of me."

"Roland's here."

"You're not bullshitting me?"

"He's here — please don't come over."

"Okay, Fletcher. I'll catch you later."

When Molly got off the phone the pizza arrived. She carried it down to the family room.

"Man, I'm starving," Roland said, grabbing a piece. "What do I owe you for my half of the pizza?"

"Forget it. It's on me — groupies always provide for the star."

"You sure?"

"Yeah."

"Who was that on the phone?"

"Oh, just a wrong number."

Six

"Molly?"

"Hmmm." Opening her eyes, she yawned and slowly looked up. "Oh — hi, Daddy," she said sleepily.

"You overslept, Mol."

"What!" She propped herself up on one elbow and grabbed her alarm clock. "Oh, no! I must have forgotten to set my alarm." She jumped out of bed.

"Is there anything I can do?"

"No — just — thanks for waking me up."

"Will you have time for breakfast?"

"No way!"

"Well, don't get too upset — you might get flutterbies in your stomach."

"That'd be tragic, Dad." Molly laughed.

"Well, have a good day." He left the room, closing the door behind him.

Molly raced around getting dressed and then ran

out to her car. Luckily, as she drove to school, she hit all the green lights but one and made it by seven fifty-five, only ten minutes late. Starting the day like that bothered her . . . why today, of all days, she asked herself, did I forget to set the alarm? Damn!

After her late start, her classes seemed to crawl by. She spent fifth and sixth period staring at the clock until the last bell at two forty-five. Roland was waiting for her at her locker. The appointment wasn't until four, but he thought they should leave right after school to avoid the usual rush-hour mess.

They walked to Roland's car, and Molly handed him the slip of paper with the address on it. "Do you know where this is?"

"I'll find it."

"Just how well do you know the east side?"

"Don't worry. I'll get you there."

"I always get lost over there — what if we never find the place?"

"Chill out, Mol. We've got lots of time."

When they arrived in Kirkland, Molly looked at her watch. "Roland, we're forty-five minutes early!"

"I wanted to make sure you were here on time for your appointment." He smiled. "I made very sure." He drove along Kirkland Way, checking the addresses. "There it is," he said, pointing to a two-story brick building near the corner. "What do you want to do while we wait?"

"You probably want to get something to eat."

"I don't have to."

"I'm not a bit hungry — my stomach's full of flutterbies."

"Flutterbies?"

"Just a family word — my dad always said that's the name of the species of butterfly that people get in their stomach. When you're uptight or in a rush — you know, nervous and stuff." Molly looked across the street toward the water. "There's a park over there. Why don't we just hang out until it's time?"

"Are you sure you don't want to get something to eat?"

"Roland, go get a hamburger, will you? I'm fine. I'll just sit in that park and wait for you."

"Okay, I happened to notice a McDonald's back there."

"Yeah, I'm sure you did just happen to notice it, and the Big Mac has been calling your name. Get outta here — I'll see you later."

Molly crossed the street and found an empty park bench facing the lake. Nearby, children were playing on the swings, climbing on the jungle gym, and running and chasing each other on the beach. Watching them was a nice diversion. Behind them, a dock jutted from the shore enclosing a small marina where the sound of sailboat riggings clinking against the masts mingled with the children's laughter. The water sparkled in the afternoon sun, and she felt the soft breeze against her face. It must be a good day for sailing.

Molly looked at the beach, then her eyes rested on two figures near the drinking fountain. At first she casually noticed the pair, but soon found herself staring. A father picked up a small girl, who was clutching a paper bag, and held her while she got a drink. Then he walked with her over to the beach, and they began feeding the ducks.

Molly's eyes were fixed on the man as he tore up the bread in little pieces just like her father used to do; Molly remembered going to the edge of the lake, throwing the bread in the water, then running back to him, a little afraid to get too close to the ducks. Afterward they would always get a hamburger at Kid Valley, and then he would take her to the lab where she could see the baby pigs.

She was startled when she heard Roland. "Didn't you see me wave? You look like you're in a trance — "

She began fishing in her purse. "Roland" — she looked up at him — "I can't do it."

"Can't do what?"

"I just can't keep that appointment. Do you have a quarter?"

He looked puzzled, but he reached in his pocket, found a quarter, and handed it to her. "Are you all right?"

"I've got to call and cancel it. I have — I'll be right back."

* * *

When Molly got back to the bench, Roland jumped up, looking worried. "Are you sure you're really all right?"

"Yes. But I just can't do it."

"What happened?"

"I don't know. I just felt all this stuff about my dad — Roland, my parents would be really hurt, my dad especially, if I got information and talked to someone at that adoption place without telling them about it first. I tried to kid myself that it was just information and not really doing anything. But it would hurt them. I just know that."

"Then do you want to tell them?"

"I have to. And I have to do it now — because I haven't been able to stop thinking about who my birthmother is and finding out what I am, and I can't stand feeling so damn guilty. Do you have another quarter?"

Roland nodded and looked through the change he had in his pocket. He handed her another quarter.

"Thanks. I'm going to call Mom — right now, before I lose my nerve."

"I'll wait here for you."

Molly walked over to the phone booth again and called her mother's work number.

"Laurelhurst Pediatric Clinic."

"Dr. Fletcher, please."

"She's with a patient right now. Can I have her return your call?"

"This is Molly, her daughter. I'll just wait on the line until she's free."

Molly heard a click while she was put on hold. She gripped the receiver tightly as she looked through the phone booth toward the lake. Roland was sitting on the bench talking to a little boy who had come by walking his dog. Roland and the little boy both patted the dog. . . . Roland was so nice to little kids.

"Molly?" Ellie Fletcher's voice was concerned.

"Hi, Mom."

"Molly? Are you all right?"

"I'm fine — Mom?"

"Where are you, Molly?"

"I'm in Kirkland and — "

"Kirkland?"

"Everything's fine, but I have to talk to you and Dad. I want to talk to you both — tonight." Molly paused for a minute. "Mom," she said softly, "it's important."

The sky clouded over on their way back to Seattle and by the time Roland dropped Molly off, the misty drizzle had become a downpour. Outside the back door she took off her wet jacket, shook it, then took it in, draping it over the kitchen chair to dry. The house was dark and gray, and she went through the downstairs turning on lights, hoping to make it more cheerful. She tried unsuccessfully to read some of the magazines on the coffee table, and finally, unable to sit still, decided to make a fire in the den.

Molly was sitting cross-legged on the floor in front of the fireplace, poking at the logs, when she heard her parents come home. Mom must have called Dad right after I talked to her, she thought. They usually didn't arrive home together. Maybe I shouldn't have called Mom. Maybe I should've just waited for the right time. But when would the time ever be right?

"Nice fire." Her father stopped in the doorway, and was joined a minute later by her mother.

"Yes, it is. It looks cozy in here," Ellie said, smiling. "I'm going to go up and change my clothes, and I'll join you two in a minute."

"Do you want me to fix you a drink?"

"Thanks, some fizzy water would be nice."

"Do you want anything, Molly?" he asked somewhat formally, on his way to the kitchen.

"I'd love a Coke — thanks."

When Paul came back from the kitchen with their drinks, Ellie had changed into her favorite pair of corduroy pants and a flannel shirt and was sitting in one corner of the couch, her feet tucked up under her. He sat next to her, and the two of them waited in awkward silence for Molly to talk.

Molly looked at the fire, feeling hypnotized as she stared at the flames. She became frozen for a moment as the flames danced and flickered over the logs.

"Molly, you wanted to talk to Dad and me tonight?" Her mother's voice finally broke the silence.

She took a deep breath and turned her back to the fire so she could see both her parents. "I want to talk to you about something I learned about this week and — I — uh — well, maybe it would be easier" — she reached in her jeans pocket where she had put the N.A.S.O. brochure — "if I just show you this."

Molly looked at her mother; all of a sudden she seemed so small, curled up in the corner of the couch. Molly handed the brochure to her father.

Taking his reading glasses from his pocket, he put them on and glanced at the outside of the brochure. "N.A.S.O. — Northwest Adoptees Search Organization," he read aloud and then looked up, his eyes meeting his wife's. He unfolded the brochure, sharing it with Ellie.

"We have speakers from different organizations come to our family psych class — you'd like it, Mom, we've had speakers from Planned Parenthood and Seattle Day Nursery and someone from Children's Orthopedic Hospital talking about child abuse, and anyway, well, this week we had a lady from the Northwest Adoptees Search Organization, and she handed out these brochures."

As her parents read the brochure, Molly's heart

began pounding so loud, she was sure they could hear it across the small room. But the crackle of the fire was the only sound. She stared at the flames and then took the poker, drew open the wire curtain screen and jabbed at the logs. The black iron rod shook when she held it with just one hand, and she had to steady it with both hands.

"Molly, what does this mean?" her mother asked.

"What does it mean?" Molly repeated her mother's question. She felt confused as she looked at her parents sitting on the couch. Her father was holding her mother's hand. They both seemed tense.

Her father spoke. "Yes. Does it mean that you want to join this group, then?" He picked up the pamphlet. "It says it's a search and support group for adult adoptees, birthparents and adoptive parents — "

Ellie looked directly at her daughter; her blue eyes were clear and steady but she gripped her husband's hand. "Molly . . . does this mean that you want to search for your biological mother?"

Molly looked at her parents. She felt like she couldn't breathe. "I don't know. I'm not sure — but I want to find out what's involved."

She sat quietly in front of the fire, looking up at her parents, her heart thumping in her chest.

"Molly, what do you want us to do?" her father asked.

"I want you — to understand."

There was a long silence, the fire crackled, and

Molly's father took a sip of his drink. The ice cubes clinked against the glass.

Her mother stared at the brochure. "The office is in Kirkland, 220 Kirkland Way." She read the address off the front of the brochure. "Is that why you called me from Kirkland today? Are you — have you gone ahead with this?"

"No, Mom." Molly's hand was shaky as she took a sip of her Coke. "Ever since I got the brochure, I've been thinking about it a lot, and I thought I'd try and get more information before I talked with you, so I made an appointment with N.A.S.O. for today after school. I drove to Kirkland, but then I couldn't go through with it — I had to talk to you and Dad first."

"I'm grateful you decided to do that. I think I would have felt betrayed if you hadn't talked to us." There was an edge to her mother's voice.

"Mom — that's the last thing I want you to feel — please don't feel that way. See, this really isn't about you and me, it's not about us — it's only about me, something I might want to do for myself."

"It says here this is for adult adoptees, for people eighteen and over. Does that mean next year, when you're eighteen, you won't need our permission — is that correct?" her father asked.

"I'm not sure. But I want you and Mom to find out about it with me."

"But would you do it anyway?" her mother asked.

"I don't know. Someday, maybe — I might — I

just don't know. But Mom, I've always wondered about my birthparents. And now I know it's normal! All these other adopted people want to find out. Can't you understand? I love you and Dad — you're my *real* parents — you're the ones who have really raised me. But that doesn't mean I haven't always wondered who I look like — don't you understand? I don't even know what I am — Chinese or Japanese or Korean or what. And about my birthmother — why didn't she want me?"

"Why does it matter?" Molly's father's voice was sharp.

Tears stung Molly's eyes. She stared at the fire. Silence engulfed the room, interrupted only by the hiss of the wet logs, and the occasional crackle of the kindling and the ticking of the mantle clock.

Molly wiped her face and looked up at her mom who was also quietly crying, her shoulders shaking, her hand covering her eyes.

"How could you do this to us?" Paul Fletcher's voice cracked. "We've done everything we could to be the best parents we could, for seventeen years, and now we get this!" He stood up and walked out of the den.

"Paul, please — " Ellie called after him.

"I — can't — talk about this — " he said through clenched teeth. "It's too much of a blow!"

Molly, with tears streaming down her face, went to her mother and buried her head in her lap. "Mom, please — please understand. I love you so much. Please understand!"

Ellie held her daughter as Molly sobbed in her arms. "I love you, Molly — " Her voice caught in her throat as her tears spilled on Molly's dark hair. "I need time — at the very least — Molly, you've got to give me some time!"

Seven

Molly tossed and turned. Her eyes were swollen from crying, and her throat still hurt. Maybe a glass of water would help, she thought, throwing back the covers. On her way to the bathroom she heard her parents' voices rising up the stairs from the living room. Moving closer to the landing, she huddled there, straining to make out their words.

"I'm so afraid . . . I feel so old. . . ."

"You're not old."

"Paul, her mother had her when she was eighteen. She's only thirty-six now — I can't compete with — "

"I don't know how Molly could do this to us. How could she? I can't make sense out of it. I don't know what we've done — "

"Do you think any of this is because Molly never seemed to really rebel like a lot of teenagers?"

"I don't know. I don't think so — it's too big. But

I can't believe that she'd do this to us — if race was such a big deal why didn't she ever talk to us?"

"I don't think that's all of it. Paul, somewhere, I've always known Molly would want to find out about her birthmother. If we had adopted a white baby, I would have thought the same thing. I wasn't prepared, though — maybe I never would have been."

"I never thought she wanted to know about her genetic mother. Why should she? We've been good parents!"

"You never once thought Molly would want to know?"

"No."

"Oh, Paul. It seems human to me — of course she would wonder."

"She's never talked about it before."

"Yes, she has. She used to ask me questions sometimes about her other mother."

"I don't remember anything about that. And I'll tell you something, Ellie — just that word 'adoptive parents' bugs the hell out of me." Her father's voice rose. "Molly's mine — she's my daughter!"

"You can't forbid her to do this, Paul."

"Maybe not. But I damn well don't have to be a part of it!"

"I might decide to be."

"You're not serious?"

"Look — I'm hurt, and I'm scared but — "

"But what? Don't you resent this whole thing!"

"Paul — shhh — you'll wake Molly."

* * *

Unable to hear anymore, Molly went back to her
room and fell into bed drained and weary. In the
morning she lay curled under the covers, listening
to her parents getting ready for work. She had been
awake for hours, thrashing about since four A.M.,
unable to stop replaying the previous night. When
her father walked out, she felt like she had been
kicked in the stomach. Even her mother had been
hurt more than she thought was possible. . . . I hate
feeling guilty for wanting to know where I came
from! What could I have said that would have made
them understand?

She drew her knees tightly against her chest, feeling small and helpless, and began to wish she could
take the whole thing back. If only I had never said
anything. She felt sick about what happened, hating
that she had hurt them.

She stayed in her room, pretending to be asleep,
until she heard both their cars leave. Then, dressing
hurriedly, she hoped she'd be able to get to school
before homeroom started so she could find Roland.
She decided she'd go straight to his locker.

Roland —
   *Last night was awful with my parents. I've
   got to talk to you. Please come over right after
   school or call me if you can't.*

                                          Love,
                                          M.

92

Molly propped the note against the shelf at the top of Roland's locker and was closing the door when she felt a hand on her shoulder.

"What're you doing up here, Fletcher?" Joe leaned against the locker, holding his leather bomber jacket slung over his shoulder with his other hand. He always managed to look cool, Molly thought, wondering if he worked at it. He leaned close to her. "Why aren't you in your homeroom like a good girl?"

"You're late, Joe."

"Yeah, we're both late. Why don't we just cut out of here? Tell our first-period teachers that we have to do some cheer squad crap."

"I can't."

"Might be fun, Fletcher."

"I gotta go, Joe."

"Sure." He turned and headed down the hall, then turned back. "My car's right by the gym door. Sure you won't change your mind, Fletcher?"

"Bag it, Joe."

What was with him, anyway? Molly left for her homeroom, wondering what it really would have been like if she had cut first period and gone with him. Probably driving to Ravenna Park for some serious groping, or maybe there was no one home at his house, and he had his bedroom in mind. Nothing would surprise her about that guy.

On her way to her first period class she bumped

into Trish Barnes who reminded her that everyone on the squad had to turn in their medical forms by the first of next week. Molly had forgotten all about it. She realized that she'd have to talk to her mom that night about getting it filled out.

Roland came over right after school. When Molly unlocked the kitchen door to let him in, Roland was waving vigorously at the house next door.

"What're you waving at?"

"I'm sure Mrs. Wiley's watching somewhere, so I just thought I'd wave."

Molly laughed. "Oh, Roland, come on in. I'm so glad you could come over — I really need to talk to you."

She took two cans of Coke from the refrigerator and handed one to Roland. "Let's go downstairs."

In the family room, Molly turned on the TV and sat on the couch next to him.

"Your note said it was awful with your parents. What happened?"

"A disaster." Molly stared at the TV. Then she got up and went over to it and turned the volume down so it wasn't so loud. She came back to the couch and sat facing Roland. "It was really bad, Roland," she said, quietly. "Mom and I both were crying, and Dad was furious — he yelled at me, then he just left."

"What'd he say?"

"He said that was all the thanks he got for raising me for seventeen years."

"Oh, God — that's what you were afraid of."

"I know."

"Was your mom like that, too?"

"No, but she was really hurt. She said she needed time."

"What're you going to do?"

"I don't know — I really don't. Just wait, I guess. Maybe Mom and I can talk."

"Do you wish you hadn't told 'em?"

"Kind of. But then I get mixed up. I wish I could just forget it for a while."

"I've got just the thing."

"What?"

"To take your mind off it. I've got something to show you — "

"Please — nothing about adoption — I don't think I can handle it."

"Nope. I said it would take your mind off it." Roland took some folded pieces of paper from the back pocket of his jeans. "Here," he said, unfolding the paper, "this is what I wanted to show you." He handed it to her. "Read this. It's the lyrics for my new song — the original stuff for the contest."

Molly tried to keep a straight face while she read:

I don't read the papers
I don't see the news

All it does, baby
Is leave me confused

But one thing I know how to do
Is stick around you and love you like glue
DO-WAH DO-WAH DO-WAH DO

Molly handed the paper back to Roland. "Roland, uh, well — I don't quite know what to say."

Roland grinned. "Great, isn't it? It's called 'Love You Like Glue.' "

" 'Love You Like — Glue'? I can't believe you're serious about this."

"Believe." He beamed proudly. Then he looked at her and scowled. "You don't like it, do you?"

"Well — I mean. I think it needs some work. 'Love You Like Glue'?" She repeated the title incredulously, then started to laugh. " 'Love You Like Glue' — ha-ha. Oh, Roland!"

"You know, Molly, when I'm famous, I'll always remember these moments with you in the early stages of my career when you kept the faith, when you kept believing in my talent, kept this unshakeable belief in me when everyone else had given up, your loyalty, your unwavering support, your — "

"In your ear, Hirada!" Molly picked up a pillow from the couch and hit him over the head.

Roland grabbed her, and they wrestled on the couch like a couple of puppies, until he lay over her holding her shoulders pinned to the couch. "All

96

right — all right. I quit!" Molly shrieked.

He looked down at her, still holding her shoulders. Then his face flushed, and he seemed confused. Quickly he released her. "That ought to shut you up," he mumbled, sitting up suddenly. Molly jumped up and turned the volume on the TV back up.

They sat not speaking until finally Roland looked at his watch. "I gotta go."

"Roland, wait — "

"I gotta pick up Justin."

"Listen, I'm sorry I laughed at your song."

"Oh, maybe it's not that great." Roland went up to the kitchen and grabbed his jacket from the chair. At the door he grinned. "But old Rockin' Roland is not through yet."

"Roland, thanks for listening — about my parents."

"I can't believe your parents won't come around."

"I wish I knew that" — Molly bit her lip — "but I'm not sure of anything anymore."

"Hi, honey — I'm home."

Molly went down to the kitchen. Her mother was taking some lamb chops out of the freezer to thaw in the microwave.

"Mom, I have to talk to you about something."

"Molly — I — " A look of hurt clouded her mother's face.

"It's not about N.A.S.O. or any of that stuff, Mom.

Here — " Molly walked over to the counter where she had left her books. She took out the medical form from her notebook. "I have to get this filled out for cheer squad," she said, handing it to her mother. "I just wondered if you can fill it out for me, or if you want me to go to somebody."

Ellie looked at the medical form, reading both the front and the back. "Well, a doctor shouldn't really practice medicine on her own family. I can make an appointment for you with Dr. Blumberg in my office if you want, honey. It's probably not a bad idea for you to have a physical anyway; you haven't had one in a while." Ellie still held the medical form. She stared at the last paragraph on the second side. Then she looked up at her daughter. "Molly — " Ellie walked over to the kitchen table and sat down. "Come and sit down for a minute, honey."

Molly sat across from her mother who placed the medical form on the table between them.

"This is really hard for you, isn't it?" Ellie said quietly, looking at the form. "Where it says 'relatives' — where you're supposed to give the medical history of your family?"

Molly nodded as her eyes filled up with tears.

Ellie reached over and covered Molly's hand with hers.

"I've been thinking about it all day." She looked across the table at her daughter. "I wasn't going to say anything until I had a chance to talk with your father — but I might as well tell you. Molly, I'll go

98

with you to talk to those people at N.A.S.O."

"You don't have to, Mom — "

"I know that."

"Are you sure?"

"I told your father last night that I always knew someday you would want to know about your birthmother."

"Mom, I just want to find out about my background — my heritage — it doesn't have anything to do with how I feel about you and Dad."

"I know that — at least I know that in my head. Emotionally it's hard, Molly." Ellie looked out at the lake. "I just don't want to lose you — "

"Oh, Mom." Molly went to her mother and put her arms around her. "I love you — you're my mom," she whispered.

Eight

"I've never resented anything so much in my life!"

"Paul, you've got to let go of this bitterness."

"I can't believe you're going to help Molly do this to us, Ellie."

"Maybe I don't feel that there's a choice."

"Of course there's a choice — what are you talking about?"

"Molly needs me, and I believe she has a right to find out the truth about her background."

"Well, I feel like it's the most incredible slap in the face I've ever experienced in my life. And even that doesn't describe it! Frankly, Ellie, I don't see how you can be so damn calm about the whole thing."

"I'm not calm!"

"Well, if you hadn't jumped into this thing so

quickly — maybe Molly would have thought twice about it!"

"God, no wonder Molly can't talk to you!"

"Oh, so now we're taking sides, I suppose — "

"Well, isn't that what you want me to do — be on your side against my child?"

Down the hall Molly was curled up in her bed listening to their angry voices. It was the second time she had heard them fight late into the night. She lay there crying quietly. They were still arguing when she finally cried herself to sleep.

In the morning, the minute she woke up she threw on her bathrobe and ran down the stairs. She couldn't stand another minute of the mess she had made. Molly wanted to catch her mother before she left for work; she was relieved when she saw her reading and having coffee at the breakfast table.

"You're down here early. What is it, honey?"

"Mom — I heard you and Dad last night. Please let's just forget it. I can't stand making all this trouble."

"I'm sorry you heard us." Her mother hesitated, looking at the letter she was reading. "Molly, Dad got up quite early this morning. When I got up he had gone, but he left this letter for me on the table. It is to me, but I think you should see it. Maybe it will help you understand him a little more." She handed her the letter, took her cup to the sink and got her briefcase. "I've got to get to work."

"Mom, I mean it. I hate that you're fighting. I think we should forget this whole thing."

"Molly, yesterday we agreed that we'd go over and talk to the woman at the N.A.S.O. office on Wednesday afternoon — and that's what we're going to do."

"But — Dad, he's so upset — "

"Your father is wrong. I know how he feels, but he's wrong, and he's going to have to get through this himself. People don't own their children, and I won't let his fears dictate to me — and that's all there is to it. Now I have to get to the hospital." Ellie kissed her daughter's cheek, then turned and left the house.

Molly fixed some cereal and read the letter.

Dearest Ellie,

I was up most of the night, trying to make sense of this situation. I found myself staring at the montage of Molly's baby pictures that hangs in the hallway. I looked at her beautiful little Asian face, her big dark eyes and that full head of dark hair. Was there ever a more beautiful baby? I remember how carefully you assembled those pictures some years ago.

I've gone over every moment of Molly's adoption. Ellie, I remember that I had proposed the idea long before you were ready to consider it. I realize that you bore the most intense pain and grief about not being able to conceive; the hope you would have if your period was even

102

a day late, hoping and praying it meant a baby. After it was determined that I wasn't the problem, you were the one who had to go through all those years of doctors, and tests and the surgeries, and feel the sadness at each birthday that went by, as it meant another year without a child, and years were running out. Six months to the day after your last surgery when you still hadn't conceived I remember your announcing that you wouldn't wait any longer, and I watched you throw yourself into the adoption of a child with all the vitality and intensity that is so characteristic of you. Then there was the fear that we wouldn't get a child, that they'd find us too old. When we recognized that we might have difficulty adopting a white baby, I never felt it was that much of an issue. I believed that if problems arose, we'd deal with them as they came, that love would conquer all. Was I so naive?

I had no idea the next two years would be so frustrating; the waiting lists, the phone calls, the interviews, the visits from the social workers. Those damn interviews. Those were the worst. And when we'd just about given up, there was Molly! What a gift, to have been given this child who came to us so helpless and tiny when she was four days old.

Ellie, have we done something wrong? What has happened? Why does Molly want to do this? Underneath my anger is terrible confusion — something, as you know, that my analytical and scientific mind does not cope well with. I can't understand any of this, and I feel so estranged from you, as you apparently do seem to understand it.

Love,
Paul

Molly took the letter up to her parents' bedroom and placed it on her mother's dresser. She felt a despairing loneliness as she looked at her reflection in the mirror over the dresser. *All I want to do is find out who I am.*

On Wednesday afternoon Molly came straight home after school and waited for her mother.

"Hi, I got here as soon as I could." Ellie was a little out of breath as she came in the door.

"Mom, are you sure you want to do this?"

She put her briefcase down and looked at her daughter. "I thought we went through this the other morning."

"I hate making trouble between you and Dad. I read that letter — he'll never understand. Things are so tense around here — it's crazy. I could go over there myself so you wouldn't have to be involved — " *Please come with me.*

"Sure, and I'll just pretend nothing's going on."

"I guess all I'm trying to say is that if you changed

your mind it would be okay." *Please come*. Molly's eyes met her mother's.

"Molly — we're going."

"Wouldn't you know it," her mother muttered, turning on the lights and the windshield wipers. It began raining as soon as they got on the bridge. Cars whizzed by, spraying water on the slick pavement as they turned off onto the Kirkland Exit. Rows of condominiums lined the shores of Lake Washington. "It seems like a different world over here, doesn't it?"

"Like a summer resort or something." Molly pointed toward the water. "That park is really nice all along the lake like that."

"I don't think I could stand the bridge traffic, though, if we lived on the east side."

When they got to the N.A.S.O. office, Molly closed the door on the passenger side and then hesitated, leaning back against it. She stared at Ellie who stood on the curb waiting for her.

"Mom — I'm scared."

"Do you want to wait a bit before going in?"

"I don't know." She held the door handle, hesitating, while shoppers passed by on the sidewalk and a car parallel-parked, backing into the space in front of Ellie's Volvo.

Molly looked at her mother. "If you want to change your mind — "

"Change my mind?"

Molly nodded.

"Change my mind about what?" Ellie asked again.

"About staying with me?"

"No, honey." Ellie went to Molly and put her arm around her waist. "I'll be here."

"I guess I'm ready to go in."

"Okay."

They went in the ground floor of the building and saw a set of glass doors between a dress shop and a deli. "It looks like we go in here," Ellie said, noticing a N.A.S.O. sign with an arrow pointing down the narrow corridor. At the end of the hallway, the door of an office was open, and Ellie stuck her head in the door.

"Is this the N.A.S.O. office?"

"You must be Dr. Fletcher." A blonde, middle-aged woman came out from behind a metal desk, offering her hand to Ellie. "I'm Diane Sadock — please come in."

"Thanks. I'm Ellie, and this is my daughter, Molly."

"Yes, I've talked with Molly on the phone," she said. "I'm glad you could both make it today." Her smile was friendly as she offered chairs to them.

Molly looked around the office. It was lined with high bookshelves stacked with phone directories from what must have been every major city in the United States. Behind Mrs. Sadock's desk, hanging over some file cabinets, was a large map of the state of Washington. Molly stared at the phone directories, then anxiously at her mother. Thank goodness she was there. *Why was this so scary?*

"I had never heard of N.A.S.O. until Molly brought home some information about it she had gotten at school — "

"We've had quite a public education program going this year."

"Well, it seems to be working." Her mother took off her sweater, placing it over the back of the chair.

"I'm sorry if it's too warm in here — "

"No, I'm fine — thank you."

"What school do you go to, Molly?"

"Roosevelt — in Seattle. A speaker came to my family psych class."

"Oh, sure, one of our volunteers — Peggie Camano — was doing school visits in Seattle last week."

"Molly got very interested, and we wanted to talk to you about N.A.S.O. and get more information — "

"That's all we want to do today," Molly spoke quickly. "Just find out how it all works."

"Of course." Mrs. Sadock nodded as she opened a desk drawer and took out some Xeroxed material, handing a sheet each to Molly and Ellie. "This pretty much outlines the procedure. We can go over it together, and I'll answer any questions you have."

When Molly was finished reading the sheet, she

went back and reread the first paragraph and then looked up. "It says the adoptee has to be eighteen — "

"How old are you, Molly?"

"Seventeen; I won't be eighteen until January."

"The only time we've waived that requirement and petitioned the court to open the records is when there is a compelling medical reason to find a birthparent."

"So, if Molly decided to do it, she would have to wait until she was eighteen?"

"Yes, but we would encourage anyone planning to search to attend our meetings to learn more what to expect and get support from the group — from the other adoptees, birthparents and adoptive parents. Every week people report on the reunions that have taken place."

"What exactly would happen when Molly turns eighteen?"

"If I decided to do it, Mom — "

"When you turned eighteen the first thing we would do is appoint your C.I. — Confidential Intermediary — they're volunteers in our organization who actually conduct the search."

"So we wouldn't be doing the search?" Her mother looked puzzled.

"No. The reason is to protect the rights of the birthmother. She may not want to let her identity be known."

"You mean I could decide to go ahead with this,

and my birthmother might be found but she might not want to know me?"

"That can happen and sometimes does — and her wishes and her privacy must be respected. The C.I. is appointed by the court; the name of the C.I. will go on the petition to the court. You see, the court is petitioned to open the adoption records in order to learn the identity of the birthmother. The C.I. takes an oath of confidentiality, and if they violate that oath they could face up to a ten-year prison sentence if they give any information about the birthmother without a signed consent form."

"So it means my birthmother has to sign a consent form before they tell me who she is?"

"Exactly."

"And if she doesn't? Then does that mean it's over — that I could never find out who she is?"

"I'm afraid that's right. But you also have an opportunity to change your mind, too, Molly. After your birthmother is found and has consented, you would be told by your C.I. and asked if you were ready to make contact. If for some reason you changed your mind, or perhaps only wanted information about your birthmother and medical records but didn't want any actual contact, that could also happen."

"Does that happen very much?" Molly had trouble imagining turning back at that point. Maybe in the beginning — but not after they found the person. Not after all that.

"Not often."

"How long does it usually take?"

"There's a three-month waiting period until you can be assigned a C.I. — actually we could initiate that three months before your eighteenth birthday to speed things up, if your parents signed a consent form — then the court is petitioned, and the records are opened to the C.I. The C.I. begins the search then. But after that we have no idea how long it would be. Were you born in the United States, Molly?"

"Yes — in Seattle. I mean, that's what you always said." Molly looked at her mother.

"She was born in Seattle."

"When adoptees are born in other countries the process is more complicated and frankly, there are fewer reunions. But the younger the adoptee is, the better the chances are that the search may be much shorter. The record keeping is much better when you don't have to go back so far."

"What are the reunions like?" Her mother's blue eyes looked steadily at Mrs. Sadock but Molly noticed she clasped her hands in her lap, nervously twisting her wedding ring back and forth on her finger.

"I wish I could tell you that they're all wonderful, but the only thing I can say with certainty is that they're all different. For some adoptees, the reunions have been disappointing, although I must say that even with those, I've never met an adoptee who

110

regretted having searched — just finding out the truth seems to satisfy such an important need. But quite a large number have been very happy for everyone."

Mrs. Sadock paused for a moment and looked at Molly's mother. "A happy reunion does not create another mother-child relationship — I can't stress that enough. And it really helps to talk to other adoptive parents about this. If it's a happy reunion it's like finding a friend, and much of the happiness for the adoptee comes from finding out the truth; it's a feeling of finding a missing piece, of completing something. That's how I felt."

Molly looked over at her mother. She was beginning to feel overwhelmed. She wanted to ask Diane Sadock more about what it was like for her to find her birthmother — but not now; her head was swimming.

"Are there costs involved for N.A.S.O. to conduct a search?" Ellie asked.

"There's a membership fee and a search fee that come to $150.00. It is a big decision." Diane Sadock looked at Molly. "Some adoptees who've had reunions felt that making the initial decision to search was the hardest part. But feel free to come to our regular meetings — it may help you in sorting things out and deciding what you'd like to do."

"Mom?" Molly hesitated; they had been driving back to Seattle in silence, each absorbed in her own thoughts. "You've never known anything about her, have you?"

"No, honey. I would have told you if I had known anything. All I know is that she was eighteen years old when you were born, and that she was in good health, and that she was Asian."

"It never said if she was Korean or Chinese or what?"

"No. I don't think your birthmother wanted anyone to know anything about her. We could never find out anything about your biological father, either; the social worker told us your birthmother said he was unknown."

"You've told me that before, haven't you?"

"Yes. I can't remember exactly when, but it was one of those times you asked me about your other mother."

"Mom, this is sort of hard to talk about, but I've just been wondering so many things. Could she — could she be retarded? I mean, could a person who was mentally handicapped in some way have a normal baby, a baby with normal intelligence?"

"Yes, it's possible."

"Or what if she's crazy? She could be in a mental institution. A crazy person could have a normal baby, couldn't they — insanity isn't inherited, is it?"

Ellie drove down 25th past the Husky Stadium. "Molly, there are some mental illnesses, manic-depressive illness for instance, which have what is

112

called a genetic predisposition — that just means that sometimes there can be a tendency in families for the members to be more prone to developing that illness than in other families where it doesn't show up. But that does not mean that mental illnesses are in any way specifically inherited."

"But she could be crazy — she could be in some mental institution somewhere."

"I guess almost anything is in the realm of possibility."

"If I do this, Mom, I'd have to be prepared for something that might be really awful. She could be a prostitute or in prison, even."

Ellie reached over and patted Molly's hand. "Molly — if you decide that you must know who she is, if you choose to go ahead with a search, whatever you find out, bad or good, has nothing to do with who you are. If she turned out to be any of those things you are afraid she might be, it would have absolutely nothing to do with the kind of person you are.

"Molly — I know you're almost eighteen, and you will have the right to do this, but I have to say that I would want you to be absolutely sure that you understood that your birthmother is no reflection on you at all — you must know this before you start a search for her." Ellie turned the car into the driveway, and parked it in the garage. She looked over at her daughter. "This is important Molly; I don't want you to get hurt."

Nine

Molly helped her mother fix dinner, and they ate as soon as her father got home. The three of them were tense and formally polite with each other. *Please pass the salad. Thank you. How was your day? Fine. And yours? Fine, thank you. May I have the potatoes? Sure. Thank you. What's on TV tonight? I don't know. We'll have to check the paper. More coffee?*

Finally Molly couldn't stand it. She put her fork down. "Don't you even want to know what happened at N.A.S.O. today, Dad?"

"I really don't have anything to say about your genetic mother."

"Why do you always say that — that 'genetic mother' crap? She's a real person, there's a real person who carried me for nine months and gave birth to me — not just a mess of genes!"

"Molly, please . . ."

114

"Forget it, Mom. I'm sorry — but I've got to get out of here." She left the table and ran up to her room.

Molly called Roland. Irritated, she tapped her fingers on the table, waiting for him to answer. When he finally did, she could hardly understand him.

"Roland? Is that you?"

"Sorry," he said, swallowing. "I was chomping down a pizza when the phone rang. You know, speaking of pizza, you and I are very compatible. We both like pepperoni. I was helping Megan Lee with her geometry the other night and we got pizza. She likes Hawaiian pizza — that garbage with Canadian bacon and pineapple. That's not real pizza, in my opinion."

"In my opinion, I do not want to hear anything about that bimbo."

"Sorry."

"I think she's a sleaze."

"Uh-huh."

"Do I talk about anyone who might be interested in me?"

"No. Didn't I just *say* I was sorry. Lighten up! Now listen, you gotta hear my new song. It was inspired while I was watching the Cleveland Browns play the Oilers on Monday Night Football." He cleared his throat, then wailed into the phone:

Sitting in the dog pound, howling with the crowd.
Throw a bone at my baby. Man, it's gettin' loud!

115

She's sittin' on the fifty with another guy.
Bark at my old lady, see them biscuits fly!
Woof! Woof! I got the dog pound blues —

"Oops, Mol, there's a beep, I've got another call coming in."

"Oh, forget it, I just had a very heavy day, that's all, Roland," she snapped as she hung up.

Molly immediately called Kathy and was relieved to find her at home. Kathy wanted to know all about how things had gone for Molly and her mother at the N.A.S.O. office — every detail, and Molly brought her up to date.

"At least you listen, Kath. I called Roland, who was stuffing food in his face — then he insists on singing his latest pathetic song. Plus, he even had the *nerve* to mention Megan Lee."

"I heard she's going to ask him to the Tolo."

"You're kidding." Molly was quiet for a minute.

"No way. She's really psyched to ask him. She's been all over him. Who are you taking?"

"God, I haven't even thought about it, I've been so hung up with all this adoption stuff."

"I can see why you haven't thought about it — with all that going on. Unfortunately I've had to think about it a lot. I was assigned to write a thing for the newspaper about how girl-ask-guy dances are called 'Tolos' in the Northwest. Other places they call 'em 'Sadie Hawkins' dances. Tolo's an Indian name —

116

it means achievement of success. Would you like to hear all the facts about this?"

"I'll read the paper!" Molly laughed. "So who're you taking?"

"Kevin Herrera, I guess. Why don't you take Joe?"

"Joe Abrams?"

"Sure, he hangs around Kevin. The four of us should go."

"Damn that Roland. We always did that stuff together — I don't know why he has to screw everything up by spending time with that sleaze. I just don't get it — not that I care."

"So ask Joe — "

"You know that I am very tired of being *such a nice girl* and all that junk. It's nauseating." Molly hesitated. "But that doesn't mean I'm ready for someone like Joe Abrams. I've really got to think about that one, Kath."

The morning of the N.A.S.O. meeting Molly woke up early thinking about her father. What could she say that would make him understand? He was still refusing to even talk about the fact that she and Ellie were going to the meeting that night. Maybe she should make one last try. It couldn't hurt anything, she guessed. Molly lay there wondering what she could say or do, then jumped out of bed and rifled through the top drawer of her desk until she found the quote from *Roots* Roland had given her.

Carefully, she copied it, then underneath it she

wrote a note to her father. She read it over, rewrote it, read it again and finally went downstairs and left it by the coffeepot.

In all of us there is a hunger, marrow-deep, to know our heritage. To know who we are and where we have come from. Without this enriching knowledge, there is a hollow yearning. No matter what our attainments in life, there is the most disquieting loneliness.
— Alex Haley

Dad —
Please come to the N.A.S.O. meeting tonight with me and Mom. I need you, and I love you.
Your daughter,
Molly

That evening, her father didn't say a word about getting the note. It was time to leave for the meeting, and Ellie was getting her coat out of the hall closet. Molly stood in the doorway to the living room and zipped up her jacket, watching him as he just sat there, reading the paper.

"Dad, did you get my note?"

Paul Fletcher put down his newspaper. His eyes filled with pain.

"Molly — don't push him!" Ellie spun around.

"Mom — I — "

118

"This is hard, Molly. Do you understand that! It's just damn hard!"

"But I thought — "

"Listen, sometimes I resent this, too. Your father is not the only one having a hard time with this. I may believe you have an absolute right to do this, Molly — but that doesn't mean that my feelings are all tied up in a nice neat little package, and that I don't have any problem with it!"

"Well, then, let's forget it! I'll go myself!"

"No. That's not the point — just because it's hard doesn't mean it shouldn't happen. I can get through this, Molly — but I need your reassurance as much as you need mine."

Molly started to cry. "Oh, Mom — " She hugged her mother and they stood in the hallway, holding each other.

"You'd better get going," Paul said, "or you'll be late." He took the newspaper and went in the kitchen.

It was cold and rainy. Fall was ending and the drizzly gray days of Seattle winter came with more and more regularity. "I'm glad I wore my winter coat," Molly's mother said as they got out of the car in front of Pier 66 at the waterfront. She glanced at the building. "I haven't been in the port building in years. I actually never realized anyone but the port commission met here."

They went in the main door and found their way

119

to the elevators. A night security guard directed them to the commission room on the third floor.

"This place is huge," Molly whispered, surprised to see what seemed like a hundred chairs in the large room. Diane Sadock spotted Molly and Ellie standing in the doorway and walked over to them. Thank goodness, a familiar face, Molly thought. An attractive red-haired woman who got off the elevator after they did came up and joined them, and Mrs. Sadock introduced her. "This is Mary Robinson. She's one of our C.I.'s."

Molly was surprised at how young she seemed. The title "Confidential Intermediary" sounded so official. Not that Molly was sure what she had expected — maybe someone with a briefcase and a lot of papers and a badge or something. Mary Robinson was wearing jeans. As they chatted, Mrs. Sadock told them that Mary was a graduate student at the U.

Then she looked at her watch. "I've got to go get things started."

Molly led the way to three chairs in the back row. "This looks like a good place to escape from if we need to." Molly laughed nervously, glancing at her mother.

"I think my parents would have preferred to leave the car motor running the first time." Mary smiled. "Now they come all the time." She pointed to a couple near the front. "They're sitting with some other adoptive parents over there."

The meeting started with some general announcements, then the newcomers were asked to stand and introduce themselves. After that, the group heard a number of members report about the successful reunions that had occurred since the last meeting.

Mary leaned over and whispered, "Not all searches are successful, and some reunions are not happy — like the ones you're hearing about tonight."

"I don't even know yet if I want to do a search."

"For a lot of people, the two hardest times are making the decision to search and then after the reunion. There's a real let-down — it's really kind of an anticlimax, no matter who you find."

They listened to the minutes of the last meeting, reports of the legislative committee, the education committee, and then the recap of last week's reports on all those who were searching. Molly looked around the room wondering which adoptees were having their names read, which names belonged with which faces. Would they be reading my name someday? She looked anxiously over at her mother, trying to find some sign. *How was she taking all of this?*

When the meeting ended, Mary asked if they could stay for a few minutes. "I'd really like you to meet my parents."

"Is it okay, Mom?"

"Sure. I'd like to meet them."

"I'll be right back." Mary headed through the crowd as Molly and Ellie went to get coffee.

"What do you think, Mom?"

"I don't know — I suppose I have a lot of mixed reactions. What about you?"

"I'm surprised how matter-of-fact people are about it."

"Being here certainly makes you aware of the feelings of all the people: the adoptees, the birth-parents and the adoptive parents. That one birth-mother who's searching for the child she gave up, she seemed so discouraged, I felt sad for her." They got some coffee and made their way back to where they had been sitting.

Mary returned with her parents and introduced them. The Robinsons were both as warm and out-going as their daughter. While Ellie talked with them, Molly and Mary went to get coffee refills. "I wish I knew how Mom is reacting to all this," Molly said when they were out of earshot.

"It will probably help her to talk to my parents. You know, I really do envy people who are involved in open adoption. You wouldn't have to decide to search; everyone would just expect to meet, with it all out in the open from the beginning."

Molly kept glancing over at her mother in the corner of the room. "I don't know how to get it across to Mom that it doesn't have anything to do with how I feel about her."

122

"Maybe there isn't anything you can say that will reassure her. Believe me, if I knew what you could say to her that would help I'd tell you — but it may be the kind of thing a person just has to experience."

"My dad doesn't want any part of this. My wanting to just come here and find out more about it has really screwed things up at home."

"That makes it hard, but it really is typical at first. All the parents are so afraid they're going to lose you if you find your birthmother, but the ironic thing is that I've never felt closer to my parents as when I had the reunion with my birthmother. I had never needed or appreciated two people so much in my life."

"How long did the search take?" Molly stopped glancing across the room at her mother and looked intently at Mary.

"Well, it took about eight months for my C.I. to find her. She had been married and divorced and then married a second time and she lives on Vashon Island out near the lighthouse at Point Robinson."

"Where did you have the reunion?"

"We decided to meet at the beach by the lighthouse, but on the day we were going to meet it was just pouring, so we met in the N.A.S.O. office instead. Diane arranged for me to have the key so it was really private, just Mom, Dad, me and Terri."

"Terri." Molly repeated the name.

"You seem surprised."

"I don't know — birthmother is a word, and you know it means a person and all, but when that person has a name — I don't know, it just kind of hit me, I guess. What was she like? What was it like meeting her?"

"She's a potter, and her husband's a commercial fisherman. We look a lot alike — I guess that was the first thing that felt so unbelievable. Molly, it's hard to find words to describe what it was like, but when I met her, something in my life was completed."

"Do you see much of her?"

"We have lunch every once in awhile. Sometimes Mom joins us. I like her, and she's a good friend, although we're really in different places in our lives." Mary drank the last of her coffee. "The main thing isn't whether you get a new friendship out of the deal — although that's nice when it happens, but the main thing is finding out the truth about who you are."

Molly nodded. Talking to someone who understood was incredible. She felt close to Mary Robinson even though they'd just met.

"The fact that your mom is here is really good. Maybe your dad will change his mind." Mary went through her purse looking for a pen and wrote her phone number on a slip of paper. "This is my number — just give me a call whenever you want."

"Thanks a lot." Molly hesitated. "If I ever get this figured out — well, Mrs. Sadock said you were a C.I.

I just wondered if, well, can you request a specific person?"

"Sure."

"So you could be my C.I. if I wanted?"

"I know there'd be no problem with that at all. We'd just need to tell Diane Sadock." Mary looked through a notebook she was carrying. "Here — I've got something else for you." She handed Molly a small sheet of paper. "This really is kind of sugary and sentimental, but the sincerity of the person who wrote it does come through. It's an anonymous poem titled 'Legacy of an Adopted Child.' "

"Thanks. I'll give it back to you at the next meeting."

"No need — I have a lot of copies." She looked over at Molly's mother. "Molly, one bit of advice."

"Sure."

"About your mother. It's really overwhelming for them at the first meeting. She made a big step tonight and, well, I just wouldn't push anything right away."

On the way home Ellie was quiet. Molly was uncomfortable, but she tried to take Mary's advice. Just shut up, she told herself; Mom will probably talk about the meeting when she's ready.

Before she went to sleep, Molly put Mary's phone number next to the phone beside her bed. Then she read the poem Mary had given her.

Legacy of an Adopted Child

Once there were two women
Who never knew each other
One you do not remember,
The other you call mother.

Two different lives,
Shaped to make your one.
One became your guiding star
The other became your sun.

The first gave you life
And the second taught you to live in it
The first gave you a need for love
And the second was there to give it.

One gave you a nationality
The other gave you a name
One gave you the seed of talent
The other gave you an aim.

One gave you emotions
The other calmed your fears
One saw your first sweet smile
The other dried your tears.

One gave you up
It was all that she could do
The other prayed for a child
And God led her straight to you.

Molly had tears in her eyes when she finished reading the poem. That's me — definitely sentimental, she thought as she pulled the covers up around her.

She closed her eyes, but she couldn't shut her mind off even though she knew she had finally made a decision. Why did I drink all that coffee? she wondered. Now I'll never get to sleep. She snapped on the light and went down to the kitchen to get some milk. As she went down the stairs she heard the low murmur of her parents' voices coming from the kitchen.

"Are you going to tell Molly?" she heard her mother ask.

"Tell me what?" Molly came in the kitchen and glanced up at the kitchen clock, pulling her bathrobe tight around her. "Don't you guys know it's the middle of the night?"

"We couldn't sleep — sorry if we woke you up. Want some coffee? It's decaf — " Her mother gestured toward the pot.

"I came down to get some milk."

"Molly, Mom and I have been talking — and, well, I did a lot of thinking tonight." Paul Fletcher hesitated, then looked at his daughter. "If you want to do this, this search for your birthmother — I — uh, well, I'll try and go along."

Molly nodded as her eyes filled with tears. "I asked Mary Robinson tonight if she could be my C.I., if I decided to do it. The way I understand how this works is all I have to do is call Diane Sadock and request it and then have you two sign the consent form, so the search could start in January when I'm eighteen."

"That's just a few months," Paul said quietly.

"But tonight as I was lying awake, I decided that unless you both were willing to help me, not just sign the form, but be with me through the whole thing, then I couldn't do it. I might have someday when I was a lot older, but not now — not without both of you."

Her father reached over and held her mother's hand. "Molly, tonight while you and Mom were gone — I don't remember the house being emptier. It wasn't like you were just out shopping, you know." He smiled sadly. "After you left, I watched the news on CNN, and on the 'News from Medicine' segment they reported that in some kidney transplants now they've had some success using other donors when a blood relative can't be found."

Molly looked puzzled, but said nothing as he continued.

"I guess I needed to be confronted with a reason to do this that I can understand." He spoke carefully. "If you ever needed a blood relative — if your life depended on it, I'd do anything to help you. I'll also tell you quite frankly" — he glanced at Ellie — "I was afraid of being left behind."

"Oh, Paul," she said quietly.

"One thing about me, when I make up my mind,

that's usually it. I don't obsess about things much — "

"No, that's my department." Ellie smiled.

" — and I don't look back. I don't pretend to understand the way you feel, Molly, the way your mother does, but I have something I can hang on to."

"That you're going along with this in case I might need a blood relative to save my life someday?"

"That's right. It's what makes sense to me, and the way I've always operated is that if I can find something that makes sense to me then I can make my peace with it."

"Whatever works, that's all I can say, and thank God you've come around, because I don't think I could get through this without you, Paul."

"We need you, Dad," Molly said softly.

Paul held out his arms, and Molly went to him. He held her for a long time until finally she spoke. "I'd like to call Mrs. Sadock tomorrow," she whispered, her dark head buried in his shoulder. "Okay?"

"Okay . . . my Molly Jane."

Ten

"Roland, you won't believe what happened!" Molly ran up to him at his locker. "Last night, we went to the meeting, and I met this really neat person, and Mom was there, and she's going to be my C.I., and we met her parents" — she grabbed his arm — "and then the best thing was that my dad came around — you just won't believe it, and I've already called that lady — "

"Whoaaa — " Roland closed the door to his locker. "Take it from the top."

"Huh?"

"Slow down, you know — nice and easy, one word at a time, I'm not dumb, but — "

"No one said you were dumb." Molly looked exasperated. "Did I say you were dumb — ever?"

"That's because I'm Asian, just another one of those model minority mental giants, smart, smart, smart."

"Smart ass."

"Now it's verbal abuse!" Roland pounded his fist on his locker. "Why do I put up with this?" Then he saw that Molly wasn't laughing, that she looked upset. He put his arm around her. "Hey, do you want to start this conversation over?"

"Okay."

"I'll walk you to your next class — where you goin'?"

"French — in 302."

Roland kept his arm on her shoulder as they went up the stairs. "Okay, so you went to the meeting last night, the N.A.S.O. meeting, right?"

"Right."

"And your mom went with you, right?"

Molly told him what had happened.

"So this morning I called Diane Sadock, the director of N.A.S.O. She's sending Mom and Dad consent forms so my C.I. can be assigned before I turn eighteen. Then when she gets those back signed, she'll assign me to Mary Robinson, and she'll petition the court to open my records when I do turn eighteen."

"Wow — that's in January, not that far away."

As they passed the chemistry lab, Megan Lee poked her head out of the door. "Roland! Hi — wait up! I've got to talk to you."

Roland stopped. "I guess I'd better see what she wants. I'll talk to you later, okay?"

"Don't count on it." Molly snapped. She stomped

131

down the hall, not looking back. Right before she went in her French class, she turned and saw Megan with her arms around Roland's waist, standing against the lockers looking up at him. That sleaze. She acts like no one exists but him. Where does she get off hanging all over him like that? Molly wondered if she had been so preoccupied with all the adoption stuff that she had totally missed the fact that Roland was actually getting involved with that person.

At lunch she found Kathy in the student council office where she had been meeting with the senior class officers. The meeting was just breaking up when Molly got there.

"Come on in." Kathy motioned to Molly. "I'm *so* pissed — the senior class officers are just nerds. We might as well not have any."

"How come?"

"There's not going to be a senior fall Tolo because those nerds say they don't have time to organize it because of applying to colleges, so they're just going to postpone it until spring."

"That's weak."

"I'm the only one that wanted to work on it, and I'm not going to do the whole damn thing by myself."

"Yeah, I don't blame you."

"Frankly, not having a Tolo is the least of my problems — everything's going down the toilet. The band's falling apart." Kathy sounded upset. "Did Roland tell you about it?"

"Roland and I must not be as tight as we used to be — only it seems I'm the last one to know. It looks like he's involved with Megan Lee, and he's really being a jerk because he hasn't even said anything to me about it."

"I don't think he's going with her. But she is definitely after him; she uses every excuse she can to be with him."

"This subject depresses me. What were you going to tell me? What about the band?"

"God, talk about depressing. This Saturday the band was going to meet at Susie Hildebrandt's house to make the basement tape for MTV. We were going to use her parents' video equipment, but it seems it's broken, and no one cares enough to chip in to rent some."

"That's terrible. I know Roland must care — he's been writing songs for it."

"They're terrible."

"They are. They're terrible." The bell rang, and Molly grabbed her books. "I'm really sorry about the band."

"It's worse than a garage band. It's a joke band."

"I've got to get to P.E." Molly put her hand on Kathy's shoulder. "I'll talk to you later."

Molly ran down the stairs to the gym. At least it was only P.E. she'd be late for and being on the cheer squad usually meant an automatic "A" in P.E. anyway. Next semester should be a lot better without

133

everyone being so uptight about every single grade since all the college applications would be in. In a way, she couldn't blame the class officers for not wanting to do all that work on the senior Tolo. Especially since every one of them was trying to get into Stanford or Harvard or somewhere like that. Trying to figure out where to apply was bad enough, and then the S.A.T.'s were coming up and then having to fill out all those applications. It *was* a pain.

"Hey, Fletcher — " Joe came out of the guys' locker room. He was wearing sweats but he had his shirt off with just a towel wrapped around his neck. He took the towel off, whipped it around her waist and pulled her to him. "Gotta get some practice in handling your body before the next game."

"Get out of here, Joe."

He yanked the towel and she fell against his chest. "Gotcha."

"I'm really impressed with how strong you are. Is that what I'm supposed to say?" She tried to sound sarcastic, but her heart was racing as she felt the warmth of his skin. "Do you mind?" She put her hands on his chest and pushed, but he held her tight against him. "This Rambo crap sucks, Joe — I've got to get to P.E."

He laughed and let her go, then snapped the towel against her butt as she ran into the locker room. "I usually get what I want, Fletcher."

That jerk, Molly thought. Who does he think he is? She felt shaky as she changed into her P.E.

134

clothes. She wished she weren't so affected by that guy. Could he tell how shook up she was? She hated to give him the satisfaction of thinking that she was turned on by him. But the truth was . . . she was. How stupid. It made her feel ridiculous and like a little kid. Here she was, nice Molly Fletcher scared to death because some guy was hustling her. At least she had told him that Rambo crap sucked, at least that was a little less like nice, nice Molly. She should have flipped him off.

After school, Molly was at home looking through *Lovejoy's Guide to Colleges* but was having trouble concentrating. She kept thinking about Joe, then Roland and Megan Lee. All the colleges started sounding alike. She didn't know how she was ever going to figure out where to apply. At five-thirty she heard her mother's car in the driveway and went downstairs.

Molly opened the door just as Ellie was putting her key in the lock. "Here, let me have that." She took a grocery sack from her mother.

Mabel Wiley opened an upstairs window and poked her head out. "Where's Ronald? I haven't seen much of him lately, Molly Jane."

"IT'S NONE OF YOUR BUSINESS, MRS. WILEY!" Molly grabbed her mother's hand, pulled her in the house and slammed the door.

"Molly! You yelled at Mrs. Wiley!" Ellie started to laugh. "You know, I've wanted to do that for years."

135

"The old bag deserved it. It's about time we fought back. One of these days I can see myself opening a window and yelling out at her, 'I'm mad as hell, and I'm not going to take it anymore!' "

"Poor old soul, she really doesn't understand how annoying she is. But I honestly don't think she's malicious, just intrusive." Ellie started unpacking the groceries. "I stopped at Safeway on the way home. I got a beautiful piece of salmon."

Molly put the milk cartons in the refrigerator. "How was your day?"

"Pretty good, really. But I'm seeing a lot of different viruses now that we're well into the flu season. There isn't much to be done for most of them except treat the symptoms." She took some apples from the grocery sack and began washing them in the sink. "Did you have a good day?"

"I called Diane Sadock first thing this morning, and she's sending you and Dad the consent forms."

"So we should get them tomorrow or the next day."

"Yeah." Molly sat at the kitchen table. "I guess my day was okay, except — well, this dumb girl is interested in Roland. Not that I care, really."

"He's just your friend, right?" Ellie winked.

"Mom — that's all!" Molly bristled. "It's just that this girl — she's the kind of person who'd sleep with anyone. Then today I was wondering if my birth-mother was like that. Maybe it'll end up that the only thing I appreciate about her is that she didn't have

136

an abortion. And that's confusing because I don't think having an abortion makes someone a terrible person. I've always seen things the way you do on that. But Mom, you obviously must be pro-adoption, too. I mean, which *are* you for, anyway?"

"It's not a question of being pro-adoption versus being for abortion rights, Molly. I don't see it as an 'either-or.'" Ellie turned off the water and dried her hands. "My position has always been that people don't have the right to impose their religious beliefs on other people. Women should have the right to make their own choices, that's all."

"Could my birthmother have had an abortion, I mean, was it legal when I was born?"

"Not in this state, but of course, women had illegal abortions and some went to other countries where it was legal at that time, like Sweden and Japan."

Ellie went to Molly and put her arm around her, touching her face to the top of Molly's dark hair. "Thank God your birthmother decided to have you. Thank God. That's all I can say."

Eleven

"Molly?"

"Is that you, Mary?"

"It's me."

"Just a second, let me turn down the stereo." Molly put the phone down. "Hi, I'm back, sorry. I could hardly hear."

"How was your Christmas?"

"Really wonderful, and my birthday was even better. Mom and Dad took me and my friend Kathy Barksdale — I think I've mentioned her before — anyway, they took us to Mt. Hood in Oregon to go skiing. We had the best time."

"Speaking of your birthday, that's actually why I'm calling." Mary hesitated, clearing her throat. "It's happened. We took the petition to court." There was a long silence. "Molly?"

It was still silent.

"Molly, can you hear me?"

"It really is happening, isn't it?"

"It really is, that's right. The judge should sign the petition to open your records by the end of this week at the latest. Then I'll start the search next week. Also, Diane Sadock is sending you the ISSR registration form; it's a form for the International Soundex Reunions Register, which is an international clearinghouse for people hoping to find lost relatives."

"I remember hearing about that at the last meeting. I'm glad Mom and Dad and I went to those every month. It's helped."

"Well, I just wanted you to know where we are."

"How long do you think it will take? I know that's a ridiculous question, I know the answer by heart from the meetings: 'two hours or two years — or not at all,' but I can't seem to help asking."

"If you can, just try to forget all about it because there's just no way of knowing."

"Was this part hard for you?"

"It's incredibly frustrating to know your C.I. has the name of your birthmother, but that you can't have any information unless she's found and gives consent. It almost gets harder somehow. I know that."

"Can you at least tell me how the search is going?"

"I can, but honestly, Molly, my experience is that the best thing is for you to really try and forget it. It's too disruptive otherwise."

* * *

As soon as Molly got off the phone with Mary, she called Kathy, but Mrs. Barksdale said she'd gone downtown. Her parents were out so she called Roland. She knew he'd understand what a big deal this was.

"Hi."

"How come you never call me anymore?"

"Roland. Do you realize how ridiculous you sound? Here I am, calling you up, and the first thing you do is give me a bad time about it."

"Whenever I call you, your line's always busy."

"So's yours."

"How could it be? We have call waiting."

"I did not call you up to have this conversation — "

"I guess I am in a crappy mood."

"Could have fooled me. What happened?"

"My manager at work is not giving me the hours I need to work around practice and the game schedule."

"That's terrible! What are you going to do?"

"I don't know. I need the money, but there's no way I'd give up basketball."

"So why not get another job?"

"You just don't walk in a place and demand certain hours. It doesn't work that way. I don't want to talk about it — it's depressing. How are you, anyway?"

"Well, it's happened. I just got off the phone with

140

Mary Robinson, and she sent the petition to open my birth records to court, and the judge will sign it by the end of the week."

"It's hard to believe — I mean, it doesn't seem that long ago that we first drove over to that place."

"I know. It might not be that long before I find out what kind of Asian I am."

"That's really important to you, isn't it?"

"You know it is."

"Sometimes I get fed up with the image Asians have."

"Like what?"

"Oh, you know, that model minority crap. That Asians are all smart, hardworking, family types. I think it's a nerd stereotype, and if you don't fit it you're super weird. Like my family . . ." His voice trailed off.

"Are you talking about your dad?"

"Sure. The guy leaves, never sends my mom the money he's supposed to — I haven't even seen him since last summer, and that was for about an hour as he went through town on his way to some job in Alaska. I'm not even sure it's worth inviting him to graduation because I doubt he'd show anyway. Some family guy — he's a model asshole."

"I'm sorry, Roland."

"No big."

"Do you want to come over?"

"I gotta go to work — oh, just a second — I got another call. Do you want to hold a minute?"

"No. That's okay. I'll talk to you later."

"Molly?"

"Huh?"

"That's great about the court thing and all — "

"Yeah."

"Thanks for telling me about it."

"Sure."

Molly was sure — there was just something in his voice when Roland got the call on the other line — that it must have been Megan Lee. We used to share so much stuff, almost everything, in fact, Molly thought. Why had everything changed? Damn.

It seemed too lonely hanging around the house so Molly decided to drive over to Green Lake and walk around the lake. The trail around the lake was always crowded with people jogging, walking and riding bikes, the whole place overflowing with kids and babies and dogs. It always cheered her up.

Near the boat house at the north end of the lake she saw an Asian woman walking a little toy poodle, a little puffy dog with a red bow on its head. Could that be her? With that dog? She never had liked those nerdy little dogs. Molly realized she had been worrying about the worst thing, that her birthmother was in prison or a prostitute. But maybe she was just someone that Molly would have nothing in common with, or maybe just some jerk, like Roland's father.

Could her birthmother have gotten mixed up with someone like that? Then Molly was struck with a jarring thought: What if Roland's father was her father? They'd be brother and sister, after all! *That's just too bizarre*, she decided. This whole thing is getting weird. Mary's right, she should just try and forget it.

"Hi, you're just in time." Ellie was taking a fish out of the oven for dinner when Molly got back from Green Lake.

"That looks so good."

"Dad and I were down at the market. The King salmon looked so superb, we couldn't pass it up."

"Wow, this is quite a feast," Molly said, sitting down at the table. "I'm glad you guys are home; I've been wanting to talk to you all afternoon."

"We're going out after dinner." He took a bite of the salmon. "This is great, Ellie."

"We've got Sonics tickets tonight. What's up?" her mother asked.

"Mary Robinson called me right after you left. And they took the petition to the court."

Ellie put her fork down and took a sip of her water. She looked at Paul.

"Also, Mary said Diane was sending me something called the ISSR registration form to fill out. Now that I'm eighteen that can go ahead, too."

"Molly, let me get this straight. They went over this at the meetings, but I feel a bit blank for some reason. This really means now that the records will be open and the search will begin."

"Yes. Mary said the records could be open at the

end of next week, and that she'll begin the search right away."

"And it means your birthmother could be found right away — next week — or maybe not for years, is that right?" Ellie asked quietly.

"Yes. Or maybe never."

"But it's possible they could find her right away," her father repeated.

"Yes. Diane Sadock told me about a search where the birthmother had listed her uncle as next of kin on the hospital admission form, and the C.I. looked in the phone book and called the uncle, who gave the C.I. the birthmother's phone number. The C.I. called the birthmother and a reunion was arranged the next day."

Ellie pushed her chair back from the table and began taking off the dishes. She went quickly to the kitchen, turning her back to Molly and Paul. She turned on the water and began scraping the dishes. She cleared her throat. "We'd better get going to the game, Paul," she called from the kitchen.

"I wish you didn't have to go. I feel like I'm about five, only there's no baby-sitter coming." Molly laughed. "It's been kind of a heavy day. But Mary says the best advice is to just try and forget about the whole thing. So I guess the Sonics should be good for that for you guys."

"What are you doing tonight?"

"Kathy's coming over. We'll probably just rent a movie or something."

144

"Well, have fun."

"You, too."

Upstairs, Molly knocked on her parents' door. She'd had trouble getting the VCR to work right, and she wanted to ask her dad about it before they left. When her mother opened the door, Molly saw that she had been crying.

"Mom — what's wrong?"

"I'm trying, Molly, God knows, I'm trying. But this is all happening so fast, and when you told us how there was a reunion that happened the next day — the very week the records were opened. That could happen to us! It could be sometime next week — that's so fast!"

"Oh, Mom — " Molly didn't know what to say.

"I just feel pushed, that's all. Even though I knew all this stuff from the meetings, I don't know — this whole thing is hard enough. Then when it starts bothering me again I start feeling guilty that I'm not being understanding enough."

"Ellie, you've got to calm down." Paul tried to reassure her. "Let's just go to the game and forget about all of this for a while. We can talk to Mary's parents and see how they got through this first part."

"So now you're the rational one — " Ellie smiled and blew her nose.

"It's my turn to be."

"It's going to be okay, Mom." Molly went over to

her mother and hugged her. "Really it is," she said, trying to convince herself as much as her mother.

The next week Molly tried to take Mary's advice and forget about the search but her efforts were met with varying success. On Wednesday, she arrived home to find her mother in the kitchen.

"Mom, what are you doing here?" The warm kitchen smelled of freshly baked cookies.

"My last patient was at three, and I usually get caught up on paperwork on Wednesday afternoon, but I decided to come home. Here — " Ellie motioned to the baking sheets on the counter. "Have some. I just took them out of the oven."

"These look delicious. I love the chocolate chips warm and gooey like this. . . . Aren't you having some?"

"Sure. I'll get a cup of coffee and join you." Ellie got her coffee and sat across from Molly at the kitchen table.

"You haven't made cookies in years. In fact, mostly I remember that we'd buy the dough in a plastic roll, and I'd end up eating the dough. I don't think the cookies got made much." Molly laughed.

"Yes, as you'd say these are serious cookies. Made from scratch."

"They're wonderful."

"Good."

"It's weird having you be here — I mean, having

you be home when I get home from school."

"I can leave and go back to the office. I certainly have plenty to do there."

"No, I don't mean that, but Mom — listen, about these cookies — "

"What's wrong with them?"

"Oh, Mom. That's not the point, it's about the lunches you've been making, too. Every morning this week I've found a lunch that you packed in the refrigerator — "

"What is the point, Molly?" Her mother sounded hurt.

"I'm just worried that you're doing all this stuff because the search is starting."

"Well, I — "

"Listen, Mom. I love you. You're a doctor and — "

"I've always worried — not being a traditional mother."

"So what?"

"That my career might have hurt my family, and now if you find her — "

"I'm proud of you — there's nothing wrong with the way you are, and I don't need cookies or my lunch made. I just need you to be you." Molly looked tenderly at her mother. "I'm not trying to find her because you didn't bake cookies."

"It's terrible that you just ate the raw dough from the plastic roll — "

Molly started laughing.

"What's so funny?"

"I'm worried that the lady's going to be a hooker — and you're afraid she's BETTY CROCKER!"

Twelve

Thank goodness, the sun's out, Molly thought as she left for the Roosevelt-Garfield track meet. She decided she'd better make this one; Garfield was their big rival. Everyone on the cheer squad seemed to lose enthusiasm in the spring, the track meets never got big crowds, and just one or two cheerleaders would show up as a token gesture of school spirit. Molly didn't go that often; like most seniors on the squad she really wasn't into it.

Kathy spotted Molly when she walked onto the track, and she ran down from the bleachers. "Molly, I gotta tell you something before you hear it from someone else." She leaned close to her. "Roland's going to the Tolo with Megan Lee."

"You're kidding!" Molly looked around. "Listen, I don't want anyone to hear us. Let's go up to the top of the bleachers. No one's up there." The warm spring sun felt good on her legs as they climbed the steps.

"Now you've got to figure out who to ask," Kathy said as they sat down.

"I didn't think Megan Lee was hanging around him that much anymore. Besides, Roland's been so busy between his new job and basketball that I didn't think he had time for anyone. I thought she'd given up — I mean, *I've* hardly talked to him in months." Molly looked glumly down at the track.

"And if you haven't seen that much of him how could she, right?"

"Well — "

"Yeah, well, she asked him, and he said 'yes,' so if you want to go to the Tolo — you'd better ask someone pretty soon. It's only a few weeks away."

"I almost forgot about it — I've been working so hard this semester. Being put on the wait list at Dartmouth was the pits — it put so much pressure on me to get grades this semester. It's stupid because Dad's not so sure he wants me to go there, anyway."

"That's where he went, isn't it?" Kathy asked.

"Yeah, and he used to really want me to go there, but when they had this big mess with some racist slimeball students that they let in the place, Dad went nuts and wrote the president and everything, and now he said he's not sure he wants me there."

"I know I'm in the U — so I don't have to worry about all that."

"I'm starting to think I want to stay in the state. Whitman is my second choice, and the acceptances will be out any day. If I get in there, I think it might be better for me to be closer to home — you never know what might happen about my birthmother."

"You haven't heard anything, have you?"

"No. I don't think about it that much; we've all kind of forgotten about it — it's too weird otherwise."

"Molly" — Kathy sat up straight — "there's Joe. See? He just walked in, and he's at the edge of the track over there. Why don't you go down there and ask him?"

"He's probably already going with someone — he's always with some girl."

"No one has asked him — I know it for a fact. Besides, guys like Joe never get asked right away just because everyone thinks they're probably already going. So ask him."

"Right now?"

"Yeah, go for it! What d'ya have to lose?"

"Virginity." Molly laughed. "Can't believe I said that."

"It's about time you got rid of that. What the hell — live a little." Kathy laughed. "Listen, seriously, Joe's not a bad guy. He's a teacher's assistant in my physics class, and he's great with the kids that don't get it. He's really nice to them. Never puts them down or anything."

Molly was quiet. Maybe there was more to Joe

than just what she'd seen of the guy. She turned to Kathy. "Roland's really going with Megan Lee?"

"Absolutely."

"All right" — Molly took a deep breath — "I'll do it."

"Now."

"I have to do it now?"

"Yes — before you lose your nerve." Kathy gave her a shove. "Go on. I'll wait here for you."

Joe was leaning against the fence, cheering for the Roosevelt girl who was leading the pack in the hurdles. He had on shorts and a T-shirt. That guy has more muscles than ever, Molly thought. Probably because of gymnastics — he must be working out with weights a lot or something.

As she got closer to him, she started sweating, and her heart raced. This is crazy, why had she told Kathy that she'd ask him? Molly stopped, pretending to be engrossed in the meet. She hated being scared like this. Was she always going to be so terrified of guys? What was wrong with her? Could it be what she had suspected for a long time, that she was afraid she'd be like her birthmother? That she'd get mixed up with some guy, get pregnant and not keep the baby?

Mary told her that it was common for a lot of young women adoptees to get pregnant, as if they had a compulsion to connect with their birthmother by recreating the one indisputable fact they knew about her, that she'd had a baby. . . . She looked back at the stand; Kathy was motioning to her, pointing toward Joe. Molly glanced down the track toward him.

All she really knew about the guy was that he came on strong. That and that he was so good-looking. Maybe he wasn't that wild; Kathy seemed to think there was more to him than just hustling girls. Was Roland the only guy she'd ever feel safe around? And now he was going out with Megan. That really burned her — to think that he'd actually said "yes" to that girl. It made her so mad.

What the hell, she thought. I'm sick of always being on the sidelines. She headed toward Joe.

"Hi, Fletcher." Joe waved.

"Hi, we're doing great, aren't we?" She smiled nervously.

"The guys aren't doing as well as the girls but, yeah, we look pretty good. So you've been cheering them on?"

"Uh-huh. I'm really not that into it."

"You should come to a gymnastics meet. You'd turn me on — I'd make it to state." Joe put his arm on her shoulder. "What d'ya say?"

"Get serious for a minute, okay? I've got something to ask you."

"Anything, ask me anything."

"Well, if you're not going — I mean, well, I won-

153

dered if you'd like to go to the Tolo?"

"With you?" Joe put his hand on the back of her neck and leaned close to her.

Molly looked around. "There's no one else around here. Do you see anyone else? Of course, with me — I mean, unless you're already going with someone then forget it."

"I'd love to go with you, Fletcher. I was surprised, that's all. I've always seen you at the other ones with Roland Hirada."

"Yeah, well, it's our last year and all. Time for a change." Molly looked back at the stands. "Listen, I've gotta go."

"Hey, not so fast." He grabbed her arm. "The Tolo's a few weeks away. I think we ought to go out at least once before that, and get to know each other better."

"Well, I don't know — "

"Don't tell me we're going to go through all this again."

"Okay — I guess so."

"I'll call you."

"Okay."

When Molly got home Mrs. Wiley was in her yard, weeding the flowerbeds. She stood up when she saw Molly's car.

"Ronald was just here, Molly Jane. You just missed him."

"His name is Roland."

154

"He doesn't come here so much, does he."

"I guess not." (What business is it of yours, you old bag?) Molly walked quickly toward the house.

Mabel Wiley leaned over the hedge. "You two have a fight or something?"

"See you later, Mrs. Wiley." (If we did, a nosy old biddy like you would be the last person I'd tell.)

"Is that your phone I hear?"

Molly ran in the house just as the phone stopped ringing. She threw her books down next to the phone and stomped up the stairs to her room. When she got there the phone rang again.

"Where were you?"

"What d'ya mean, 'Where were you?' "

"I was just over there."

"So Mrs. Wiley told me."

"Why the hell did you ask Joe Abrams to the Tolo?"

"Roland, I don't believe you. I really don't — I've hardly seen you for ages, and you call me up out of the blue and start dumping on me. And you're going with Megan Lee — so what's it to you?"

"You didn't ask me — what was I supposed to do, just tell her no?"

"Well, what was I supposed to do when I found out you were going with her — stay home?"

"You didn't have to ask the biggest stick man in the class!"

"Don't be crude."

"You could have asked a nice guy."

"Like who, for instance?"

"Like Don Cirello or Sean Wing or Charles Washington — just to name a few."

"Yeah. All your friends. As if Megan Lee were some saint or something."

"Well, I never thought you'd be this stupid."

"My thoughts exactly, and there's no point in continuing this conversation." Molly slammed the phone down.

She was so mad at Roland that when Joe called her that night and asked her to go to a kegger Saturday she said she'd go — then immediately regretted it. "Just chill out, Mol," Kathy said, when Molly told her how uptight she was about going out with him. "You're in charge. Joe will behave."

Saturday night Molly tried on every sweater she owned. They all looked terrible. She wished she had never told Joe she'd go out with him. Everything from her closet was piled on her bed in a huge heap. She stood there staring at it. Maybe her mother would have something she could wear.

"Mom — " she called down the stairs. "Can I borrow one of your sweaters?"

"Sure. Which one?"

"I don't know — can I try them all?"

"Okay, take your pick."

"Thanks."

Molly found a navy-blue cardigan with gold buttons in her mother's drawer. It was huge on her, but she liked sweaters big anyway and felt calmer wearing it. It seemed to give her confidence, and make her feel secure. How stupid, she thought, dressing up in your mother's clothes so you feel like a grown-up lady. But she wore it, anyway.

Joe met her parents and was very smooth, shaking hands with both of them and doing the whole polite meet-the-parents number. On the way to the car he put his arm around her. "They really surprised me."

"Huh?"

"Your parents." He opened the door for her, then went around and got in the driver's side.

"What about them?" Molly buckled her seat belt.

"Well, the way I had it figured — because of your name and all. I thought your dad was white and your mom was Asian."

"Wrong."

"So you're adopted or something?"

"Yeah."

"What's that like, anyway?"

"People stare sometimes because I'm Asian and they're white, and I think most people think I was a Korean orphan or something because most Asian kids with white parents were from Korea — "

"So you weren't from there?"

"Well, I wasn't born there. I was born here."

"So you weren't one of those starving Korean orphans I was supposed to think about when I didn't want to finish my dinner."

"I'm just Asian, Joe — okay?"

"Yeah, no offense."

At the party, Molly sat next to Joe and sipped her beer. The stuff tasted awful. She just took one so he wouldn't hassle her about it. She was really so sick of that goody-goody image he stuck her with. But he didn't need to know she wasn't really drinking it.

"Where did you apply?"

"Dartmouth, Whitman, and Lewis and Clark." Molly took a fake sip of the beer. "What about you?"

"Stanford, Pomona, Berkeley, and U.C. Santa Barbara."

"You must like California — actually I can see you there."

"What d'ya mean?"

"Oh, you just look the part; I can see you hanging out at the beach playing volleyball with a bunch of blondes."

"I like dark-haired women." He took the beer from her hand and put it on the table. "Come on — let's dance."

"Okay."

He pulled her close to him and put his arms around her waist. "Relax, Fletcher — you're so tense." He massaged her neck and her back. "See, isn't that better?"

"Massage parlors are sleazy."

He threw back his head and laughed. "You're fun,

you know that?" He pulled her into the corner and bent down and kissed her. His lips were warm, and she found herself responding to him.

"It's hot." She pulled away from him. "Let's get our beer." They went back to the couch, and Molly grabbed her beer off the table. She took a little sip. It surprised her she had liked kissing him so much. She touched her cheek with the back of her hand. It felt really warm. I must be bright red, she thought. Good thing it's so dark down here.

Joe kissed her a few more times during the party, each time a little longer. In the bathroom she looked at her face in the mirror, and she was right; she was bright red. It couldn't be the beer. She was still nursing the same one. It's bad enough that Asians get so red from drinking but does kissing have to do the same thing? I might as well be wearing a sign that says, "Joe Abrams turns me on." It was definitely not cool.

Molly decided to ask him to take her home. Her red face scared her. It was as if something was happening to her that she had no control over.

In her driveway he leaned over and kissed her, but this time his tongue explored her mouth, and he slipped his hands under her sweater. He smelled of beer, tasted of beer, and she thought she would choke.

"Joe — " She drew her head back. "I've got to go in."

"Okay. If you have to — "

"I do." Molly put her hand on the door handle.

"One more." He held her face in his hands, kissing her softly, then hard. Then he let her go. "I'll look forward to that Tolo."

It was too late to call Kathy, but Molly called her the first thing the next morning.

"I couldn't wait to talk to you — I would've called last night but I got home so late."

"So — how was it?"

"Kathy, in the car — he was all over me. I kissed him some at the party — "

"Was it nice?"

"Well, yeah — it was. But maybe I'm supposed to be a nun or something."

"They don't have Unitarian nuns."

"So I'll turn Catholic. Listen, this guy is too much for me. I didn't like it at all when he started to get a lot more physical. And do you know what he said?"

"What?"

"There's always the Tolo."

"Hmmm — more to come, huh?"

"Yeah. I'll be fighting him off all night. And he drinks too much, too. He said he was okay to drive, but I couldn't really tell. I just wish I had never asked him."

"Are you mad at me?"

"No."

"I kind of pushed you into it."

"Yeah. But I didn't have to ask him. Damn that

160

Roland. I wish he hadn't screwed everything up —
going with Megan Lee."

"Listen, Molly — I was just on my way out the
door. Mom's car is getting fixed, and I've got to take
her downtown. Let me call you when I get back,
and let's see what we can figure out about Joe."

"Okay, thanks."

Molly put a record on her stereo and opened the
window that looked out over the backyard.

The plum tree next to it was a sunburst of pink
blossoms, and in the yard the azaleas looked like
flowering flames of coral, red and orange. She loved
spring. She went in the bathroom and turned on the
shower. She was just getting in when the phone
rang. Maybe Kathy had gotten back early.

"Hello."

"Molly, this is Mary Robinson."

"Oh, hi, Mary."

"Molly — " There was a long pause.

"Mary? Are you there?"

"Molly — Molly, I'm calling to tell you that — that
I've located your birthmother."

Part Two
Karen

Thirteen

Karen glanced in the mirror and tried to brush back the remains of her bangs, which were now a clump of black hair insisting on jutting across her forehead like a dark flag. She had been trying to grow her hair out ever since the move, but without much success. The style had been fine at home, somewhat like a crew cut in front with the back longer and cut on a sharp angle. But she could tell from the first day they had arrived in Halifax that it was definitely too trendy for this place.

She put down the brush, and looked at her watch, wishing Robbie would hurry and come straight home. Usually it was great to have him go to someone's house after school. Not only did it make her happy he had so many new friends, but it also gave her more time to work. Thank goodness it had been so easy for him to adjust. She was grateful for that, but it certainly was a contrast to how she was doing.

Her work required isolation, and although the studio was the first thing Mike helped her set up, practically before the kitchen, she still had yet to connect with a community of other artists. Before they left Vancouver, she hadn't realized how much she had come to count on that — that and so many other things; the essential diversity, the rich mix of nationalities, the wonderful food, the creative urban edge of the place, and the people, just so many different people. She even rather liked the old joke about it, that Canada had been tipped on its side and all the nuts had rolled into Vancouver.

Karen looked again at her reflection in the mirror. She certainly stuck out in Halifax enough as it was — there were so few Asians compared to Vancouver, and she thought she probably didn't need to add to it by having a bizarre hairstyle. But maybe this was a silly hairstyle to have any place, even at home. Too punk, too New Age, too much like a kid. Was that what she was trying to hang on to? At thirty-six maybe it was time she should be trying to appear more sedate. Her mother certainly thought so.

She went to the kitchen and looked out toward the street. No sign of Robbie yet. Then her eyes surveyed the backyard, which was making a valiant effort to recover from the winter when it had served as a small hockey rink for Robbie and his friends. It had been such a wonderful father-son project for him and Mike. Karen had fun watching them planning and building it. Robbie had always been told

166

about the backyard rink Mike had as a kid growing up in Toronto, but it had never been cold enough to make one like it in Vancouver.

Spring had come late to Halifax this year, as it had in most of Nova Scotia, but the fact that the backyard rink was now a muddy lawn didn't mean that hockey season had ended for Robbie Matsuda. When the rink disappeared, he just took up ball hockey. Robbie's room in their rambler home was, in itself, not unlike the rooms of thousands of other boys across Canada, a monument to the Great Gretzky. When Gretzky had been traded to the L.A. Kings, Robbie had been devastated. In his best ten-year-old handwriting, he wrote the prime minister in Ottawa, the mayor of Edmonton, and put a black armband on his Edmonton Oilers jersey with its famous number 99. He'd used black electrician's tape for the armband. "Why'd he have to marry that lady in California?" Robbie had protested. "I hate girls. They wreck everything!"

Robbie was wearing his number 99 Oilers jersey when he burst in the kitchen and headed straight for the refrigerator.

"Robbie, eat your snack in the car. They've got Betsey down at the dog pound, and we've got to go bail her out before they close."

"Again? Oh, no! Where'd she get out this time?"

"I don't know yet. We can look together after we get back, but we really have to get going. If they have to keep her until tomorrow — "

"I know — it'll be more money," he said in a singsong voice.

"It is a big deal; it's already her third offense. It'll be forty-four dollars! Hurry up. I'll write Gramma a note in case she wakes up while we're gone."

She went to the car while Robbie finished making a peanut butter sandwich and got Betsey's leash.

Betsey was a creature of uncertain heritage. She seemed to have a lot of black lab and some German shepherd and perhaps collie in her family tree. She had the gentle, sweet disposition of a lab as well as the lab's bad habit of retrieving the neighbor's garbage. The shepherd background gave her a fierce bark and an interest in digging holes under the fence, while the collie contributed to a white chest and a very shaggy coat, most of which seemed to end up all over everyone's clothes and the living room furniture.

Karen watched Robbie run in the house, thinking that even though he was only ten, she really did need him to help her at the dog pound. All those animals waiting to get homes — she couldn't stand the place.

"Who do you think called on Bets?" Robbie hopped in the car with the leash.

"We don't really know for sure if anyone called. The Animal Control truck could have been cruising around and seen her."

"I'll bet it was Mrs. Krups — "

"We shouldn't accuse anyone, and besides that

we are in the wrong, you know. There is a leash law in Halifax, and when Betsey digs her way out of the yard and is on the loose, we've broken the law."

"I hate Mrs. Krups. I just know it was her. Betsey never did anything to her — I never thought her daffodils looked so hot anyway."

"Robbie, you don't know. Maybe this time no one called. Now — what are you going to be today? Betsey's knight rescuing her from the dungeon— "

"No. I was the knight last time. This time I'm the sheriff of Clayton Park. I've come to positively identify her and spring her from jail. My men in the posse have made a mistake and captured the wrong critter," he said with authority.

Robbie swaggered into the Halifax Animal Shelter, his thumbs hooked through the belt loops of his jeans. "Howdy," he drawled. "Y'all got m'dawg — eh?" he said to the clerk, who knew the Matsudas well by now.

"Hi, Robbie. Betsey's here."

"Where'd ya git 'er this time?"

"Near Mount St. Vincent University."

Robbie was clearly in control of this part of the rescue as he followed the clerk to the cage where Betsey was confined. Karen stayed back and wrote the check, trying to shut out the noise of the animals.

Betsey was frightened and shaking but she greeted Robbie with great slobbery kisses. Her kisses made it difficult for him to snap the leash on her collar, but once he had calmed her enough to get it on they piled in the backseat of the station wagon, and Robbie began his lecture to her.

"The Animal Control trucks are green and white, Betsey," he began, gently stroking the old dog's head. "The dogcatchers wear special blue suits. Whenever you see the green-and-white trucks and the people in the blue suits, you must run, Bets — very fast, run for the hills and hide or the blue suits will get you." Betsey still shook from the trauma of her confinement but her panting was punctuated with more slobbery kisses for Robbie. "Run, Bets, run," Robbie said earnestly, "or they will put a net over you and take you away." Then Robbie pointed to passing cars in an attempt to teach Betsey what was green and what was white. Karen smiled, glancing at them in the rearview mirror.

When they got home, Robbie and Karen inspected the yard together and discovered that Betsey had made a hole, almost a trench, on the east side of the yard near the garage.

"I just don't think backyards are meant to double as hockey rinks."

"Oh, Mom — that's not the reason — "

"Robbie, I could plant things — bushes and small shrubs around the fence, and it would be harder for Betsey to get out."

"She'd still get out, Mom. She just likes to dig."

"You and Dad will have to fix it, but he's not going

to have time tonight. We're going to a party at the Durshams' and — "

"What am I gonna do?"

"Gramma will stay with you — and Robbie, be sure and keep Betsey in while we're gone, or keep an eye on her if you let her out. Dad won't be able to do anything about that fence until tomorrow."

Karen wasn't that excited about attending the Durshams' party. There had been frequent company get-togethers ever since Mike's division at Canaco Oil had been transferred to Halifax, and Karen was getting tired of the sole topic of conversation: the off-shore drilling off Sable Island. It wasn't that she was bored with Mike. His stability and calm provided a solid center for her life, and most of the time their differences enriched their relationship. She was just bored with the Canaco people.

Karen and Robbie finished inspecting the yard and went back in the house. Robbie left to watch TV, and Karen went to the kitchen where her mother had already started dinner. She was glad to see she had gotten up. It was a long trip out from Vancouver, and although she had been visiting since the end of last week, she still seemed to be having trouble adjusting to the time difference. And, too, Karen knew, at sixty-six her mother was slowing down.

"You start the meat." Her mother motioned to the refrigerator.

"Okay." *Amazing how she orders me around in*

my own house. Karen opened the door of the refrigerator where she had put up her favorite Peanuts cartoon from *The Chronicle Herald* (a paper also known in Halifax as *The Comical Herald*). It summed up her idea of what the world was about better than anything she had seen lately. In the cartoon, Charlie Brown's sister, Sally, was standing in front of the classroom giving a report to her school class: "This is my report on people. There are good people, there are bad people, and there are medium people. This is the way it has always been. This is probably the way it always will be. I'm too young to worry about it."

Mother is a medium person. And I, of course, am a good person. But she always makes me feel like a bad person. This is the way it has always been. This is probably the way it always will be.

Karen grabbed the skillet that was hanging on the wall and put it on the stove. Out of the corner of her eye she watched her mother's hands fly over the cutting board as she sliced the vegetables. She'd be real competition for a Veg-O-Matic, almost in the Cuisinart class. Karen guessed whatever dexterity she herself possessed had gone into her art and not the kitchen. Cooking was not high on her list of fun things to do. It was good Mike liked to cook as much as he did. But having Mother here was a real treat for him. He thought she made miso soup, the real thing with fresh tofu — not the package junk, almost as good as his mother's; the ultimate compliment.

He was also crazy about the sukiyaki she was making and Mother loved pleasing him — this was the third time since she'd been here that she cooked sukiyaki. Karen was sick of it.

When she heard the garage door go up, Karen turned the stove down and went out to talk to Mike. It would be better to intercept him in the garage to break the news about Betsey right away, and not when he got in the house in front of Mother. She'd be sure to butt in and take Mike's side in the inevitable argument.

He was as exasperated as she thought he'd be. "Karen, we have now spent — let's see, with today's fine it comes to two hundred twenty-five dollars on that dog, and she only cost five in the first place!" Mike grabbed his briefcase and shut the car door.

"You can't put a dollar value on Betsey! She's a member of the family. I don't like paying those dumb fines, although I can rationalize it because at least I know the money is going to feed some puppy or something that might get adopted."

"I do not go to work every day to earn a salary to support the local dog pound."

"If you and Robbie would just fix the fence better maybe this wouldn't happen! That stupid hockey rink seems to make the yard sink."

"Oh, all right." He sighed. "Look — let's not go into all that. I'll fix it tomorrow. Do you mind if we quit yelling about this in the garage? I really would like to go in the house!"

"I just didn't want to tell you in front of Mother."

"I know. Listen, what time will dinner be ready? We have to be at the Durshams' at eight."

"Pretty soon." Karen followed him in the house.

In the kitchen Mike smiled at his mother-in-law. "I smell sukiyaki. Food's great since you got here, Yuri."

Mike took a can of Colson's from the refrigerator for his daily allotment. He was very precise about it, one beer a day. And of course, he wouldn't drink anything at the Durshams'. He was very self-conscious about turning so red after more than one drink. That B-positive Asian blood always betrayed him, and he couldn't stand the thought of being conspicuous. Karen, on the other hand, could care less if she turned purple. Frankly, Michael, I just don't give a damn, she had told him quite early in their relationship. She had overdosed on being told to worry about what people would think of her, and Mike found her cavalier attitude both intriguing and irritating. Sometimes, he said, it was as if they were a lot more than ten years apart. They were both *sansei*, third generation, but there were times he felt like they were in a totally different generation.

"What time should Robbie go to sleep?" Yuri asked, winking at Robbie as his parents were leaving for the party.

"About ten." Karen noticed the conspiratory wink.

"Have fun with Gramma, Robbie." She kissed him good-bye.

" 'Bye — have fun," Mike called over his shoulder.

Karen watched Robbie and her mother wave to them from the doorway as they backed out of the driveway. She felt stupid being jealous of her own son. But Robbie had such a good relationship with Gramma. She was so loving and playful with him. Why hadn't she been like that with her? She wondered if her mother was so wonderful to Robbie because he was a boy or if it was just because he was a grandchild. As an only child, Karen didn't have much basis for comparison. She supposed she'd never know, but it bothered her just the same.

The Durshams were renting a house near Point Pleasant Park in the south end of Halifax on Point Pleasant Drive. It was an elegant neighborhood with large, stately homes. As they pulled up in front of their house, Karen had a strong wish they were back in Vancouver instead of going to what would undoubtedly be a stuffy party.

Mike put his arm around her as they walked up to the Durshams' front door, sensing her reluctance. "Don't worry. We won't stay that long."

"Oh, I can handle it."

Once she was inside and had greeted everyone, Karen was cornered by Gena Bowman who jabbered away about a Japanese flower-arranging class she was taking. Karen could never figure out why some people insisted on talking to her about this kind of thing, or bonsai trees and tea ceremonies — things she knew absolutely nothing about. It irritated her that they couldn't seem to get the picture that she was the third generation in this country and might not hang around the house having tea ceremonies. Karen excused herself and headed for the food. Oh, well, at least she hadn't been stuck in a conversation about the oil drilling yet, she thought.

She was checking out the smoked salmon, crab-stuffed mushrooms, miniature quiches, marinated shrimp and golden caviar on the *hors d'oeuvre* table, when Polly Dursham wove her way through the crowd toward her.

"Karen, you have a phone call."

Karen immediately became frightened. Something must be wrong at home. Mother would never call her at the party unless there was some kind of an emergency. Karen thanked her and went straight to Mike.

"There's a phone call for me."

"I'll come with you."

They followed Polly to the phone in the den. Polly left the room, quietly closing the door. Karen picked up the phone.

"Mom — Gramma fell down — she won't wake up!" Robbie was crying.

"Robbie? I can't hear you very well! What happened?"

"She won't wake up, Mom!" Robbie was sobbing.

Karen handed the phone to Mike. "Robbie, it's Daddy — what happened?"

"Gramma fell down," the little boy cried harder. "She won't wake up — "

"Robbie, we'll call the ambulance and be right there."

Karen reached for the phone. "Robbie, we're on our way."

"What should I do, Mom?"

"Go to Gramma and hold her hand and talk to her, Robbie — just keep talking until we get there and the ambulance gets there." Karen believed absolutely that the touch and voice of another human being might keep someone alive. "Be sure and talk to Gramma, Robbie."

"What shall I say, Mom?"

"Anything, Robbie, just talk to Gramma like you do to Betsey when she's scared."

"Okay, 'bye — Mom — " Robbie started to hang up. "Mommy, I'm scared."

"I know, Robbie, go to Gramma. We'll be there as soon as we can."

Mike had gone to the phone in the Durshams' kitchen and called the ambulance from another line while Karen was still talking to Robbie. He met her in the den, and they rushed out to their car. They'd explain to the Durshams' later.

As they left Point Pleasant Drive it started to rain. Karen's slender hand was enclosed in her hus-

177

band's. It had gotten dark out, and she gazed hypnotically at the headlights of the oncoming cars. *Please, it's not time, Mom — I — we haven't forgiven each other yet.*

Robbie hung up the phone in the kitchen and ran to the front hall where his grandmother lay at the foot of the stairs. He sat beside her, his Edmonton Oilers jersey, with its proud number 99, and the black armband smudged with peanut butter. His hand reached for hers.

"The ambulance is green and white, Gramma. The men wear special blue suits. Whenever you see the green-and-white truck and the men in the blue suits, you must run, Gramma — very fast, run for the hills and hide or the men in the blue suits will get you. They will put a net over you and take you away." *Run, Gramma, run.*

Fourteen

Karen sat in the waiting room outside the emergency room at Victoria General Hospital. She felt numb as she stared at the clock. The events of the past half hour — speeding home, waiting for the ambulance, leaving Mike with Robbie, parking the car, running to the emergency room, talking to the admitting clerk, filling out forms — they all blurred together, skewing her concept of time into a strange distortion so it seemed more like three days than thirty minutes. Her mind was playing tricks on her, it became cluttered with jarring, disjointed fragments of making grocery lists, mixing paint for the unfinished canvas in her studio, the image of her father's headstone at the cemetery in Vancouver, the telephone in the Durshams' den, and incessantly slicing through all of it — *jan ken po, aigo no sho, ma ke te mo, ka te mo, aso bi ma sho* — the sound of a child's game.

179

She froze as the doctor walked past the admitting desk and came toward her.

"Mrs. Masada?"

Karen nodded as the doctor, a tall woman resident who looked about her age, offered her hand. "I'm Doctor Johnson." She sat down in the next chair, and her voice was soft as she stumbled over Karen's name, mispronouncing it again slightly. "Mrs. Masada, your mother has had a stroke. She still hasn't regained consciousness — but she is alive and her vital signs are good."

"Will she be all right?"

"I wish I could reassure you — but it's just too soon to tell if she'll pull through it or even what the extent of the damage might be if she does. All I can say is we're doing everything we can for her. She's being transferred to the intensive care unit right now."

"Can I see her?"

"Of course. It's on the third floor."

"When will you know — if she — "

"I just can't be specific. I wish I could, truly. But we'll just have to wait." She hesitated, waiting for Karen to digest the information.

"Can I stay in her room with her?"

"Yes, of course." As she rose, she put her hand on Karen's arm. "I need to get back — but if you need anything — just ask the nurse on the unit."

* * *

Karen spent the night in the chair next to her mother's bed, dozing on and off throughout the night. At five-thirty the daylight began to break, and the room slowly filled with pale light. Karen rubbed her shoulders and neck; they were stiff from forcing her body into an awkward fetal position as she tried to sleep in the narrow plastic chair. Throughout the morning, she sat close to the bed, holding her mother's hand.

It was nearly eleven when her mother regained consciousness. Karen wept as Yuri, confused at first, mumbled, "Where? What happened?" in her first language. *"Doko? Doshitano?"* she asked helplessly, as if she were a small child. But as the morning wore on her mother began to speak in English. "Where's Daddy?"

"Daddy?"

"Uzo. Where's your father?"

"He's dead, Mom. Daddy died when I was seven — almost thirty years ago."

"Ahhh." She nodded and then seemed to become more alert. "This Vancouver?"

"We're in Halifax. Mike and I moved here six months ago — you were visiting us."

"Hai," she said softly, nodding again.

"You scared us, Mom."

"I'm a tough old lady."

Before her mother fell asleep she was able to talk clearly for a short time as the neurologist examined her. Even though she called him *sensei*, she seemed to know where she was and what was going on. After talking with the doctor, Karen went down the hall to call Mike.

"She's conscious — she's been talking to me!"

"Thank God."

"She can't move her right arm though, Mike."

"Is that going to be permanent?"

"The doctor doesn't know yet — I guess all we can do is wait."

"You must be exhausted."

"I am — but it's not bad. I just feel so relieved."

"Do you want me to come and take over there?"

"No. She's asleep now. Just tell Robbie that she's going to be okay." Karen's voice was tired. "How is he?"

"He's watching Stan the Man on *Switchback* — he says Rufus isn't funny today."

"He always cracks up over the dog."

"Not today. He doesn't think Stan's funny, either."

"I never think Stan's funny. Listen — I'm going to leave now. I'll be home soon."

The maternity ward was on the opposite wing of the hospital on the same floor as the intensive care unit. Karen passed by the nursery window on her way to the elevator and hesitated, then stopped and stared intently at the newborns. She felt a cold chill, and she pulled her sweater around her, then walked quickly to the elevator, not looking back.

182

It was about a twenty-minute drive from the hospital to Clayton Park. She thought she should stop at the Dominion in the Lesswood Shopping Centre; there probably wasn't that much food in the house. But as she drove by and saw the lot full of Saturday shoppers she didn't turn in; she was just too damn tired. She'd ask Mike to go when she got home. Maybe he'd take Robbie, and she could get some sleep.

In the garage Karen turned off the ignition, put her head down on the steering wheel for a moment, and then she started to cry. *Where were you when I was in the hospital, and I needed you — where were you?* Why had they never once talked about it? It was as if it had never happened. The shame made it something totally unspeakable for Yuri, who sent her to the states to have the baby — to the Evangeline Booth Home for unwed mothers. Run by the Salvation Army — for her salvation. No, for her mother's — it had all been arranged by Yuri and Aunt Hiroko.

Yuri had stayed in contact through letters to Karen during her pregnancy, but when Karen returned to Vancouver, after having the baby, she never mentioned it. She behaved as though nothing had happened, as though Karen had just been away on a trip visiting her Aunt Hiroko in Seattle.

Initially Karen had thoughts of her baby daily. They finally became less frequent after she married Mike and Robbie was born. But in the winter, each

January, she went through a kind of mourning, grieving for the loss of the baby, and every year for the past eighteen years on January eighteenth she said a prayer. *Please God, let her be all right*. Karen had named the baby in her own mind, even though she knew it wasn't the child's real name. It was after she first saw *The Sound of Music*. To her the baby was Julie — after Julie Andrews, who she thought had spunk and spirit and life and joy and music.

Karen lifted her head from the steering wheel and leaned back against the seat. Last night, not knowing if her mother would live — she wanted so much to feel close to her. But Yuri had never forgiven Karen for getting pregnant, and Karen had never forgiven Yuri for threatening to abandon her if she kept the baby. And they never talked about it. Instead, they settled on a civilized, polite and superficially warm relationship in which all the important things were never said.

Karen sighed and opened the car door. Slowly, she walked to the house, went in the side door and closed it behind her.

Yuri was transferred from the intensive care unit after a week to a regular ward where she stayed for another ten days. Robbie was allowed to visit a few times, and his grandmother perked up every time she saw him. Toward the end of the second week Karen became frustrated with driving back and forth to the hospital to face the daily battle she had with her mother about Yuri's insistence that she return to Vancouver as soon as she was discharged.

"Just because you can leave the hospital doesn't mean you're ready to go back to Vancouver, Mom."

"I'll feel better in my own home."

"You're not as strong as you think."

"Houseguests and fish smell after three days."

"This is ridiculous — "

"I can go to the physical therapist at home."

"You can't drive, Mom. Who will drive you?"

"I have friends — "

"You have family. We're here, and you must stay with us until you're really ready to go home."

The hardest part of the arguments for Karen was the fact that she didn't actually know how her mother really felt. So many older Japanese people, even if they had been born in Canada or the States, still communicated in a way that Karen could never quite get. They seemed to say "no" when they meant "yes," and there were all these unspoken rules that she felt she was expected to know when in fact she often just didn't have a clue. Usually, though, the nonverbal cues she could pick up. So much had been communicated that way in her family.

But this time with her mother, she didn't know if Yuri was protesting because she thought she should, or if, in fact, because she really would feel more comfortable in her own home in Vancouver. It was all so jumbled up. Why was it so hard to just be straight with each other? Did her mother think

185

she was just insisting out of duty? But so what if that was true — she would feel too guilty if Yuri went back to Vancouver before she had fully recovered. Finally, Mike interceded, insisting that Yuri stay. She agreed immediately, and that was the end of it.

The physical therapist taught Karen the exercises that Yuri needed to do to regain the use of her right arm so that Karen could take over in helping her mother when she was discharged from the hospital.

Gradually, as the weeks went by, Yuri became more able to do things for herself. Her arm improved steadily, and by the second week in May they all agreed she was ready to go back to Vancouver. Karen was relieved. It had been so long since she had been able to get anything done in the studio. She couldn't wait to get back to it.

As Karen drove home from the airport the only thing that bothered her was whether she should go to the studio right away or weed the flowerbeds. The yard had suffered acute neglect over the past weeks, and she hated the fact that the neighbors had to put up with looking at the mess it had become. She wondered if she'd ever really be able to put her work first — it always ended up last on the list after she had to take care of everyone and everything else. Maybe a studio out of the house would help; she had often talked about sharing some studio space with some of her friends in Vancouver — but that whole thing had gotten postponed when they moved. Maybe someday she'd get it together.

The phone was ringing as she went in the house. She put her purse down on the kitchen counter and ran to answer it. "Hello?" She was slightly out of breath.

"Is this Karen Kumai Matsuda?"

"Yes it is."

"My name is Mary Robinson, Mrs. Matsuda, and what I have to say is confidential." Mary paused. "Are you free to talk?"

Karen thought for a minute that she should hang up. The voice on the other end of the line seemed very far away. It was obviously long distance, and there was something strange about the call. But she stayed on the line. "Yes, I'm free to talk."

"Mrs. Matsuda, I am a Confidential Intermediary for the Northwest Adoptees Search Organization, and I've been appointed by the King County Superior Court in the state of Washington to locate you. Your daughter, an adoptee, is searching for you."

Karen clutched the phone.

"Mrs. Matsuda — are you all right?"

Seconds and then minutes passed. There was only the faint noise of long distance static and the sound of muffled sobs.

"Mrs. Matsuda?"

"Yes," Karen sobbed as she clutched the phone tightly. "Yes, I'm here — is she — is she all right?"

"Yes, she's — "

"Oh, thank God." The tears ran down her face,

and Karen clutched the phone tightly, trying to remain in control. Julie was all right. Julie wanted to find her.

"Your daughter is someone you'd be very proud of," Mary said gently.

"How did you find me? What happened?"

"Well, things are changing in the whole area of adoption reform, and in Washington an adoptee can petition the court to have the records opened, if procedures are followed using a Confidential Intermediary."

"And that's what you are?"

"Yes. I found your name through the hospital records and the name of your nearest relative at that time, Hiroko Hasagawa."

"You've talked to Aunt Hiroko."

"Yes, but she doesn't know the reason why I wanted to locate you."

"She doesn't know the baby — my daughter — wants to find me?"

"No. The only way your daughter will be put in touch with you is if you sign a consent form. That is what is required by the court."

"Does she need me? Are you sure she's all right?"

"Yes. She's fine — she's eighteen now, and she wants to know who her birthmother is and something about her background."

"You're sure she's all right?"

"Yes. She just wants to know who you are."

"I want to . . . I — I'm sorry, I, what did you say

your name was again? I'm sorry — I — "

"It's all right. I'm Mary, Mary Robinson."

Karen took a deep breath, "Mary, my mother just had a stroke — she's just left to go back to Vancouver. She's been out of the hospital a few weeks, and I have a son. He doesn't know about the baby — that I had another child. My husband knows everything, but I just want a little time to think."

"I understand. Would it be all right if I went ahead and sent you the consent form, and then you can let me know what you decide?"

"Yes, please do, and I'll call you." Karen hesitated a moment. "Mary — ?"

"Is she really all right?"

"Yes. She's a lovely young woman, and she has wonderful parents."

"Oh, thank God," Karen cried softly. "Thank you. Thank you so very much," she whispered.

Fifteen

"Betsey!" Karen called for the old dog. "We're going for a walk!"

Betsey followed her into the kitchen, jumping excitedly. Her tail swung in large arcs and thumped against the refrigerator as Karen put on her sweater and let them both out the back door. Karen headed for Sherwood Point. It was a long walk, and Betsey ran ahead, looking back every few minutes, checking to make sure Karen was still there. When they got there Karen found a perch far out on the point on one of the large rocks as Betsey bounded toward the shore. The old dog was intrigued by the passing geese and pranced back and forth at the edge of the water oblivious to the turmoil within Karen.

The wind rose in the northeast, and she pulled her sweater tightly around her. It was chilly. Even though the afternoon sun was burning off the fog along the horizon, behind her the mist still clung to the grove of pines and veiled the wind-stunted oak. Out beyond the point, the impatient cries of gulls circling a small fishing boat diligently making its way out to sea broke the silence. Then, minutes later, Karen heard a Canadian National Railway freight rumbling slowly westbound along the shore. Northwest into New Brunswick? Quebec? Ontario? Manitoba? Saskatchewan? Alberta? Would it end up in British Columbia? Strange, but she didn't feel that far from home sitting there looking out to sea. The ocean was so familiar, the taste of the salt air, the damp wind ruffling her hair; she always headed for the sea, drawn to it as if pulled there by the tides.

"Betsey!" Karen cried out.

The dog perked up her ears and ran back across the shallow water toward Karen and sat in front of her, wagging her tail.

Karen patted her head and then moved closer to her, putting her arms around the dog's neck and burying her face in her fur. "What should I do, Bets?"

The dog licked her face, which was damp with tears. Karen stayed with Betsey, patting her and holding on. "What should I do?" She tried to talk to her, but Betsey was more interested in the geese.

Karen sat staring out at the basin. She took a tissue from her pocket and blew her nose. Had it really been eighteen years? How had her mother found the Evangeline Booth Home, anyway? Probably Aunt Hiroko did the research.

Evangeline Booth — what a perfectly ridiculous name that was. It conjured up the image of temperance ladies in hoopskirts bashing up saloons and marching for other righteous causes. *Put a nickel on the drum, save another drunken bum. Save another wayward girl*.

Well, unwed mothers were a righteous enough cause, she guessed. It was such a disreputable thing, like some terrible crime then, having a baby out of wedlock — that every effort was made to protect the identities of the young women, really all just girls. Only first names and last initials were used. They stayed there about four months and then returned to their proper places wherever they had come from, leaving without a trace. Sandra T., Maryanne B. were a few she remembered and then her own name, Karen K. It was so odd for four months being known only as Karen K. When is Maryanne B. due? When is Karen K. due?

The babies were delivered either in the Home or in Harborview Hospital, and while they waited for the babies to be born, she remembered the jobs they all had at the Home. They worked in the laundry, some in the kitchen, and in their free time they played cards and worked in the craft and ceramic shops. Karen shook her head, picturing an endless sea of pottery and ceramics and the social worker who began visiting her, helping make decisions about the adoption of the baby. She had a choice if she wanted to see the child. She remembered being so afraid to see her baby. Terrified that she'd change her mind.

But what alternative did she have? Her mother said there was no choice. She would no longer be her daughter. Disowned. What a stupid, archaic, hideous concept that was. But it had been non-negotiable. She would not be allowed to return home unless she gave up the baby for adoption. Dear mother. Her sweet loving mother.

She knew it would be harder if she saw the baby, but she had to. In her memory, so much of it vague, she remembered working every day in the kitchen and falling one day . . . where? . . . when? . . . she wasn't sure but she remembered clutching her arms around her belly as she fell, trying to protect the baby.

Everyone in the Evangeline Booth Home had already decided to give up their babies. The adoptive families were waiting, and she remembered being told that a couple was waiting for her baby. She was told only that they were professionals and that they were white. Labor began and she was taken to Harborview Hospital. Karen had had a long labor, most of which she didn't remember. So unlike when Robbie was born. Perhaps she had blocked it all out. Only isolated pieces, snapshots of memory remained. She heard the baby cry, and the words, "It's a girl," and saw through a semiconscious blur a vague shape.

But later, she was told that the day before the baby was to be adopted was the day she would able to hold her. The nurse would bring the baby to Karen's room. There was one vase of flowers in the room. It had arrived with no card, but she was told that the flowers had been sent from the adoptive parents.

Karen spent hours that morning getting ready. She wanted to look so pretty, as if Julie might remember. She spent all morning setting her hair in rollers and putting on makeup. The nurse brought the baby, and the infant was crying, and Karen thought, "Good, she can holler, she's strong and fiesty, and she'll make her way in the world."

And then she held her, and the baby quieted. Her breasts, which were beginning to dry up, surged with milk, and she knew she couldn't hold her too long or she would never let go. The tiny hand curled around Karen's finger, and she wanted to put a note in the little hand, something the baby could take with her forever. I love you, that's why I can't keep you, and I'm not a bad person, and I wasn't a tramp she wanted to tell her daughter.

Two days later she was on a plane to Vancouver. At home, in her mother's house, it was as if nothing had happened. It was only mentioned once, the first night she was home while they were doing the dishes.

"What did you have?" her mother asked, while she dried one of the dinner plates.

"A girl."

"Mike, I've got to talk to you — are you through at the office? Can we meet for dinner?"

"You sound awful — is everything all right?"

"I have to talk to you. I'll take Robbie over to Timmy's house."

"Is your mother all right?"

"Yes."

"Where do you want to meet?"

"It doesn't matter."

"Well, how's The Chinatown?"

"Okay. I'm going to leave right away." Karen hung up the phone.

After she dropped Robbie off, she began practicing what she would say. Repeating different phrases, over and over, quietly to herself, trying in careful desperation to choose the right words. To make it easier? There's no way to minimize it. Better to just blurt it out. Just the facts, ma'am. *Oh God, why does this hurt so much?* When she pulled up in front of the restaurant, Mike's car was already there. It took her eyes a minute to adjust to the dark restaurant, then she saw him waiting for her at a booth in the back.

"Hi, have you been waiting long?" Karen sat down and slid across the seat.

"No. I just got here. I came as quickly as I could — you sounded so upset on the phone."

The waitress came to the table just as Karen sat down, and they ordered, just coffee until they decided. When she left, Karen told him about the phone call.

"It was from Seattle. The woman's name was Mary Robinson. She said she was a Confidential Intermediary for a group called the Northwest Adoptees Search Organization — " Karen stopped talking as the waitress returned to the table with their coffee.

Karen's hand was shaking as she took a sip.

"It's about the baby, isn't it," Mike said quietly.

"Yes."

"How old is she?"

"She's eighteen now, and — and she wants to know who I am — she wants to know me."

"Oh, Karen." Mike reached out and covered her hand with his.

Karen began to cry. "She's all right. . . . The woman — Mary, Mary Robinson says she was appointed by the court to find me — she says she's all right and — and" — Karen fumbled in her purse for a Kleenex — "she says that she is someone I would be proud of."

"Well, you haven't had much breathing room, have you — first Yuri and now this — "

"I know."

"What do you want to do?"

Karen took a deep breath. "I want to meet her."

Mike looked away, then looked down at the menu. "Are you hungry? Do you want to order?"

"No." Karen waited, hoping he would say something, anything.

"Mike — I said I . . . want . . . to meet her."

"I heard you."

"And I want you to be with me."

"I don't think I can do that, Karen, and what about Robbie? We can't let him find out — "

"NO!" Karen shouted. "NO!"

"Shh — " He looked around the room. "People will hear you — "

"I don't give a damn what people will think," she hissed through clenched teeth.

"We absolutely cannot let Robbie know about this."

Karen was shaking with rage; she grabbed her purse. "No — I will not have any more lies!" She stood up and walked quickly toward the door, not looking back.

Mike jumped up and followed her out to her car. Her hands were shaking as she fumbled for her car keys.

"Karen — wait."

"No — you listen! I have pretended that this child did not exist for eighteen years, and I won't do it anymore — not ever — not ever again. Not for you — not for anyone!"

"Karen, you could just go to Seattle, and we could tell Robbie you were visiting Aunt Hiroko — be reasonable — "

"No! I went 'just visiting Aunt Hiroko,' and I had the baby, and I've never been so alone in my life, and this time — this time someone I love is going with me. And I'm not going in SHAME! DO YOU HEAR ME?" she shouted. "I'm taking Robbie along with me, and we are going to meet his SISTER." Tears spilled from her eyes. "I left that baby once — I won't turn my back on her again!"

Sixteen

"Where have you been?" Mike was in the kitchen, fixing himself a sandwich as Karen came in the back door.

"I've been driving around."

"I've been waiting for you to come home so we can talk about this — can you talk now without getting so upset?"

"Where's Robbie?"

"He's in bed."

"I don't know what there is to say, Mike."

"Do you want something to eat?"

"No."

"Karen — can't we come to some kind of compromise about this? Why do you insist that Robbie know about the baby?"

"You know — there's no such thing as a little bit pregnant, or sort of pregnant. It's one of those absolutes in life — either you are or you're not."

"I don't understand what you're saying."

"I either sign the consent form, agreeing to let my daughter know who I am — or I don't. There's nothing halfway, there's no sort of, no in between. It's like being pregnant."

"All right — but you don't have to tell Robbie. You could sign that form and tell her who you are — even meet with her if you have to. But why the hell do you have to drag Robbie into it? It happened eighteen years ago, for God's sake."

"Just who the hell are *you* protecting, Mike?"

"What do you mean?"

"Just that — how do you know Robbie can't handle it? If he finds out someday he might resent me more — for not being open about it — for depriving him of the fact that he has a half sister."

"How would he find out?"

Karen clenched her teeth. "Because I refuse to lie! I told you that!"

"Quiet! You'll wake Robbie — "

"She may want to write to me after we meet, she might want to call sometime — I may want to stay in contact with her — I know I will! I'm not going to sneak around, hide things from Robbie. Why can't you understand! I won't do that again! What's wrong with you? I never lied to you about the baby — you knew all about her when you married me — I told you everything — "

Mike was silent.

"This isn't about Robbie at all, is it? It's about

200

Mich — you're afraid that because I loved him once — "

"Forget it, Karen, just forget it."

"I love you — this has nothing to do with you. Mich's no threat to us!"

"Are you going to tell your mother?"

"Yes. I won't hide anything from anyone — not even her — especially not from her!"

"You're being selfish, Karen."

"You know what you should have done?"

"What?"

"If you're so hung up on this — you should have found yourself some goddamn little virgin!"

Mike slept on the couch that night and left for work early the next morning before Karen and Robbie got up. After Robbie left for school, Karen got dressed in her paint-splattered jeans and workshirt and went to her studio. Plopping down in the beat-up old chair where she always sat to reflect on her work, she stared at the canvas she had been involved with for the past month. It surprised her how much it seemed to be influenced by the Atlantic — the colors were rougher, and she had used a slate blue that had a stormy fierceness to it that she hadn't noticed before.

The work had evolved so much since her early paintings with their angry political statements when she was at UBC. Those had been disturbing paintings; they made people uncomfortable when they saw so many large Asian eyes juxtaposed on barbed wire spiking shredded fragments of the Maple Leaf and the Stars and Stripes. The paintings cried out in virulent and immutable outrage against the internment of Canadian and American citizens of Japanese descent during World War II.

After she left UBC with a master's in fine arts, the creative path she traveled took her from her own *sansei* heritage to that of the North Coast native bands and the near destruction of their culture. Finally finding hope in its restoration inspired by her Haida heroes, Bill Reid and Robert Davidson, artists who were the vanguard of the renewal, her love of Haida art began to merge with traditional Japanese symbols and her later work portrayed strange and eerily beautiful cranelike ravens. How predictable it was that her mother much preferred her later work. Like many *niseis* she wanted to deny the internment camp experience. Any reminder of it reverberated wounds of profound and intense pain, and she wanted no part of any statements her daughter was trying to make on the subject. It was fine that the Japanese-Americans worked for reparations, but as far as she was concerned no amount of money could ever compensate for what her family went through, and the whole subject should be buried forever. Yuri hoped the Japanese Canadians would leave it well enough alone. Let sleeping dogs lie.

That was her mother all right: Just forget it, just don't talk about it, make anything that upset her go away just by pretending it didn't exist. Like the baby. Karen ran a hand through her hair. How was she going to get up the nerve to tell her mother? Could Mike be right? *Was* she being selfish?

She left the studio and went to the kitchen and fixed herself a cup of tea. Looking out the window at the remains of the hockey rink, she imagined what it would be like to have the eighteen-year-old girl come to visit and having to make up some story about who she was to explain her presence to Robbie or her mother; she felt a sharp wave of nausea just at the thought of it. Karen took a sip of her tea. If she was going to do this she'd best get on with it. Now or never.

As she reached for the phone, a feeling of dread flooded her and as soon she heard it start to ring at her mother's house, she almost hung up.

"Hello?"

"Hi, Mother."

"Well, Karen. What a nice surprise."

"Mom, I call you every other day."

"But you always call in the evening."

"How are you feeling?"

"Getting along quite well."

"You're not overdoing it, are you?"

"Not at all. Dr. Hayashida is very pleased with my progress. He even said a little work in the garden would help my arm improve."

"Is that what you've been doing?"

"Yes, I had just come in when you called. My

203

daffodils are coming up. It's a lovely morning here — I guess it's almost afternoon there."

"How is everyone back there?"

"Lorraine Aoki just had her gallbladder out. You know, she went in for the operation the very day I got home — "

"Is she okay?"

"Doing quite nicely. Karen, why didn't you call like you usually do when Robbie's home to talk to me?"

"Mom — there is something I want to talk with you about."

"What's wrong?"

"Please just listen to me." Karen rubbed her temples, which had started to throb. "I got a phone call from the States — from Washington. From a person with the Northwest Adoptees Search Organization."

"Oh, no."

"They said they were calling on behalf of my daughter, an adoptee who wants to locate me. The law now permits an adoptee knowledge of the identity of the birthmother if the birthmother gives written consent."

"Of course you refused!"

"No, mother. I'm going to consent."

There was an icy silence.

"Mother?"

"Oh, Karen — how can you? What about your family?"

"Don't you even want to know how she is?"

"As far as I'm concerned this person doesn't exist."

"Yes she does! I did have that baby — she's alive — she's a real person, Mother, and she's eighteen years old!"

"Then she's a young woman with parents of her own. If she got along without knowing who you are — who we are — for eighteen years, I don't see what difference it makes now."

"I want to know her — and I can't turn my back on her."

"How can you be so selfish? What about Robbie and Mike — what will people think?"

"That's all you care about, isn't it, Mother? What will people think. That's all you ever cared about. Well, I'll tell you something, Mother — I'm not a bad person — having that baby never made me a bad person!"

"I won't discuss this with you, Karen. What you suggest is unthinkable. I forbid you to do it." There was a click and the line went dead.

"I was informing you, Mother," she said quietly to the dead phone. "I wasn't asking permission."

The dial tone droned in her ears, and slowly Karen hung up.

The consent forms from the King County Superior Court, in the state of Washington, arrived in the morning's mail, and Karen had thought of little else for the rest of the day, until Robbie finally came bursting in after school.

"Hi, Mom!" Before she could answer, he raced through the house to his room and came back downstairs with his hockey stick. "I'm going over to Timmy's for a little while, okay?"

"No — wait, I've got to talk to you."

"Oh, Mom — "

"Robbie — I really have to talk to you, and I want you to stay here. Call Timmy and tell him you'll see him tomorrow."

"Aw — " But he went to call Timmy and then he went to the living room, where his mother was sitting on the couch and holding a paper in her hand.

"What's happened — is Betsey okay?" He looked around at the old dog lying on the hearth.

"Betsey's fine." Karen's heart was pounding as she looked down at the sheet of paper. "Robbie — uh — I know that you know all about babies and where babies come from and everything — "

"Oh, Mom, really," he said disgustedly. "Of course — I've known all about that stuff forever." He rolled his eyes and then went and sat next to Betsey.

"Robbie, what I have to tell you is very hard for me, but, well, a long time ago — before you were born and before I even knew Daddy — when I was a young girl I — well, I was just eighteen, and I was in love and — " Karen looked at her son who was

206

looking bewildered even though he sat patiently on the living room floor petting Betsey.

"Robbie — " she blurted out, "I got pregnant when I was eighteen, I wasn't married, and I — I had a baby — "

"You had a baby?"

"Yes and — "

"Did the baby die, like Gramma almost died?"

"No, Robbie, the baby didn't die. I went to the States, to Seattle, Washington, where Aunt Hiroko lives, and I had the baby there. Robbie, I gave the baby up for adoption. Do you know what that means?"

"I think so — "

"Well, it means that the mother who has the baby can't take care of the baby, and so the baby is adopted by parents who want a baby — then they are the parents, and they raise the baby; the baby is their child then."

"I know someone who is adopted, at least I think I do. I think David Hemple is — we were in grade five together in Vancouver; he's on the Canucks — "

"Robbie, the baby I had was a girl, and now she's eighteen, and she wants to meet me."

"Did you have a lot of babies, Mom?" Robbie was petting Betsey, and he seemed to be talking about someone else.

"No, honey. Just this baby and you, Robbie."

"The baby, did you say it was a girl or a boy?"

"It was a girl, but she's not a baby. Robbie, do you understand that this happened a long time ago, and she is eighteen years old now?"

"Is she my sister?"

"Well, yes, I guess so — I mean she is your sister, your half sister."

"What happened to her dad?"

Karen got tears in her eyes. This was harder than she ever imagined. "He left."

"Oh." He seemed very matter of fact. "Is this sister going to live here?"

"No, she has her own parents — they're her family, but she just wants to meet me, and I wanted you to know about it."

"Should I meet her, too?"

"If you want to — "

"Okay. Mom, I want to go over to Timmy's now." He jumped up and ran to get his hockey stick.

"Robbie!" Karen called after him, "we're having dinner at six-thirty."

"I'll be home," he called, running out and slamming the door.

Karen stared at the consent form in her hand. She didn't know what to make of him. Had she said the right thing? Or in the right way? It hadn't seemed to really faze him at all. She wished she had someone to talk to about whether she had done it right. Had she totally botched it? Maybe she should try and tell him again.

* * *

When Mike came home from work Karen was sitting at the kitchen table with the consent form in front of her. She hadn't started dinner. He'd probably be pissed, she thought, as she heard him come in.

"Karen?" He walked over to her and put his briefcase down. They had barely spoken to each other since she first told him about the phone call.

"Oh, hi — " she said casually, looking up at him.

"Are you all right?"

"I told Robbie."

"How did he take it?"

"Well, fine, I mean he seems fine. He didn't have that much to say, and he just wanted to leave and play with Timmy. This came today, Mike, and I'm signing it."

"It's the consent form?"

"Yes."

"I hope you know what you're doing," he said, then turned and left the room.

Seventeen

When Robbie came home from school the next day he arrived with a bunch of flowers. "Here," he said, handing them to his mother.

"Robbie? What are these for?"

"I just thought you'd like 'em."

"They're beautiful. Thank you." She kissed the top of his head as he scooted up the stairs to his room. "Let's just hope they haven't come from some neighbor's yard," she mumbled as she got a vase out of the cupboard, knowing that she didn't have the heart to suggest to Robbie that the roses just possibly might not have been growing wild.

She filled the vase with water and began cutting the flowers in various lengths. As she arranged them, she was puzzled at not hearing a sound from upstairs. He usually went bounding out of the house as soon as he got home from school, at least right after he had grabbed something to eat. Why wasn't he making any of his usual commotion? The TV hadn't even been turned on. Karen put the vase of flowers in the middle of the dining room table and went up to check on him. It was just too quiet up there.

"Robbie? What are you doing?"

"Just thought I'd clean my room." He was sitting in the middle of the floor folding his clothes.

"Rob, did anything happen at school?"

"No, Mom. I'm not in any trouble."

The rest of the afternoon, he stayed around the house, helping her make dinner, taking Betsey for a walk on the leash, and then later, after dinner, he insisted on doing the dishes, all by himself. The perfect behavior continued through the evening. Robbie even went to bed early after doing all his homework.

Karen watched TV alone. Mike had to work late. Even when they weren't getting along, she missed having him home. She hated the distance that had developed between them.

After the ten o'clock news, on her way to bed she went down the hall to Robbie's room to look in on him. As she stood in the doorway, she thought she heard him crying.

"Robbie," she whispered, going over to his bed.

Betsey was sleeping next to him, and he lay curled against the old dog crying, with his face against her head.

"Oh, honey, what's wrong?"

"Nothing."

"Robbie, please tell me — maybe I can help."

He looked up at his mother, his arms wound tightly around Betsey. He wiped his eyes on the sleeve on his pajamas. "I'm afraid."

"Can you tell me what you're afraid of?"

"If you gave my sister away — if I'm not good — "

Karen threw her arms around her son. "Oh, Robbie — oh, honey . . . how can I make you understand?" They were both crying. "Robbie . . . I gave up the baby — because I loved the baby, not because I didn't, not because she wasn't a good baby. Robbie, listen to me — let me see, Oh, God — how can I explain this?" She held him close to her and was silent. Finally she said, "Robbie — if we couldn't afford to take care of Betsey for some reason. If we couldn't afford to feed her and take care of her but we knew she could have a home where some people would love her and take care of her, then if we loved her very, very much then we would give her to those people. Do you see, Robbie?"

"What if you meet her, and you like her better than me?"

"Oh, honey, I hope I like her, and I hope she likes us. But Robbie, you're my son, and I love you. No one can ever take your place, and she has a mom and a dad who love her very much. Please don't worry. You and Daddy and I, we all love each other — it will be all right." Karen stroked his forehead and stayed with him until he fell asleep, and then quietly left the room, letting Betsey stay with him.

As she got ready for bed, she knew she had to call Seattle first thing in the morning.

The long distance line crackled, and Karen wasn't sure she was getting through. "Mary? Is this Mary Robinson?"

"Yes — this is Mary."

"Hi, this is Karen Matsuda calling."

"I'm glad you were able to get back to me so soon. Did the consent form arrive all right?"

"Yes, it did, and I've told my husband and my son. I've signed the form and sent it back to you. And I'd like to have contact with my — my daughter as soon as possible. I hope it can be worked out — my son is worried about it, and I think the most reassuring thing for him will be if we arrange for a reunion as soon as we can."

"That's usually the best thing for everyone. Would you like me to have her write or call you first? Or would you like to contact her?"

"I think I'd like to write her first." Karen's voice caught in her throat. "Mary, what is her name?"

"It's Molly. Molly Jane Fletcher."

Part Three

Children
of a Common
Mother

Eighteen

"Molly Jane!"

Molly shut the door of her car and looked up to see Mrs. Wiley calling down from her upstairs window. A quick getaway is called for here, she thought. She tossed a token wave in Mabel's direction and hurried across the lawn.

"Molly Jane!" the squeak from next door was shrill and insistent.

"Can't talk, Mrs. Wiley — I'm in a hurry." Molly quickly grabbed the mail out of the box next to the front door and whipped her key in the lock. *In a hurry to get away from you, Nose. Eat my dust.*

"Molly Jane! I must know — have you seen Herbert?"

She realized that Mrs. Wiley really was upset. Actually, it would be too bad if something had happened to the cat. It was a nice cat. Not its fault that the Nose was such a royal pain in the butt. Molly looked around the yard. "No, I haven't seen him, Mrs. Wiley. Do you think he's lost?"

"Well, it's quite peculiar." She leaned out the window toward Molly. "Herbert is the kind of cat who stays very close to home most of the time. In the spring, of course" — her voice dropped — "he does do some wandering — the birds and the bees, you know."

"How can he catch birds with that bell you put around his neck?" Molly called up to her.

"Birds and bees, dear."

"What? I can't hear you, Mrs. Wiley."

"Birdsandbees," she rasped.

"Herbert doesn't catch birds!"

"Sex," Mrs. Wiley squeaked.

"I can't hear you, Mrs. Wiley! I have to go in now — "

"SEX! I'M TALKING ABOUT SEX, MOLLY JANE!"

Molly stood on the front porch and stared up at Mrs. Wiley. The woman has lost her mind — it's happened. She's snapped. *She's yelling out her window about sex — this is totally bizarre, and I'm outta here.* "Don't worry, Mrs. Wiley, I'm sure he'll come back. I'll be sure and tell you if I see him."

Molly rushed in the house and slammed the door. How do people get stuck talking to this crazy woman, anyway? No doubt about it, she's gotten worse. She's totally nuts now. Molly put her books down on the hall table and immediately began sifting through the mail. She'd been coming straight home from school to check the mail every day that week.

There was a lot of it today — the phone bill, something from the ASPCA, more bills — Sears, the gas company, more of Mom's causes wanting money — Greenpeace, Habitat for the Homeless, Ryther Child Center, a couple of slips to pick up packages, Urban League, the L.L. Bean catalog, a notice announcing the next meeting from N.A.S.O. Would she have something to report then — about her reunion that was to take place? Was it really going to happen? She had thought of little else, and she kept going over last Tuesday's conversation with Mary.

"Molly, your birthmother called me this morning. She's consented to a reunion." The words echoed in her heart.

But Mary wouldn't tell her anything about her, only where she was from . . . that she lived in Canada, in Halifax, Nova Scotia, and her name . . . Karen Matsuda. Molly didn't even know if the Japanese last name meant that her birthmother really was Japanese or if it was her husband's name and that maybe she was of some other Asian background. She didn't even know if she was married. "It's up to her to tell you about herself." Mary had been insistent about that. So it meant more waiting. More agonizing waiting. Mary tried to reassure her. "You'll be getting a letter right away."

She was sure that's what she had heard: "right

away . . . you'll be getting a letter right away." But that was over a week ago.

Molly went to the living room where she sat on the couch and slowly leafed through the mail one more time. Still nothing. . . . Damn — why hasn't it come? She went through it again a third time — nothing, there wasn't a thing for her.

She took the mail and left it on the kitchen table for her parents and went up to her room to change her clothes. Leafing through her closet, she tried to forget about the letter that hadn't come.

She really had to start figuring out what to wear to the Tolo. The dumb dance was just a week away. Molly knew she was avoiding it because she wished the whole thing would go away. Kathy wanted to go downtown to Nordstrom's this weekend to look at dresses together. But Molly told her she'd rather go to Value Village. No joke. The idea of spending money on a nice dress that would just get messed up while she was trying to fight off that jerk Joe really fried her. Kathy insisted he had a good side, but she wasn't convinced. She was sure asking him was one of her more stupid moves of the year. Damn. Nothing was going right.

She went to the phone and called Kathy.

"Hi, what time do you want to leave for Nordstrom's Saturday?"

"I've got band practice until eleven — we're trying to get it together again. How 'bout noon?"

"Okay. Do you want me to pick you up?"

"Sure — better make it more like twelve-thirty. Molly? Did you hear?"

"Not a thing. Believe me, that's the first thing I would have said if I had. It's really starting to make me crazy."

"Do you know anything about her?"

"No. And I do understand that it's up to her to tell me herself, that Mary can't, but all I know is her name and that she lives in Halifax, Nova Scotia. I keep wondering what she's doing there — it doesn't seem like a place where there'd be a lot of Asians. You can't believe the kind of stuff I imagine about her."

"Like what?"

"Maybe she lives there because she's a druggie, and they have some rehabilitation center there like the Betty Ford Clinic in the States, or maybe she's a leftover hippie living in the woods with hairy armpits, or maybe she's this yukkie yuppie with one of those ugly Louis Vuitton purses who does aerobics all day, or maybe she's like the horrible Church Lady on *Saturday Night Live* — you wanna hear more?"

"Enough already, you're right — this is making you crazy. You should be thinking about shopping. Saturday we'll shop 'til we drop."

"What kind of a dress do you think I should get?"

"Sexy. Something very sexy."

"That's what I'm trying to avoid with that guy!"

"No — it's for Roland. He should eat his heart out when he sees you."

"Hmmm — actually, that's not a bad idea. Do you realize that we've hardly spoken ever since I asked Joe to the Tolo. He's always with Megan."

"You need to get revenge. Looking gorgeous in a sexy dress is the way to do it."

Molly laughed, and when she got off the phone with Kathy she did feel better. But it wasn't long before she started in once more with fantasies about her birthmother. *It's just not that easy to forget about it.* She had to talk to Mary, and she picked up the phone again. While she waited for her to answer, she looked out the window at Mrs. Wiley's yard where Mabel was looking in all the bushes and calling for Herbert.

"Mary — it's Molly."

"Hi — did you get the letter?"

"That's why I'm calling. I haven't heard anything yet. Is there anything you can tell me — just anything at all?"

"Molly, this is one of the hardest times. I feel like I have to respect her right to tell you about herself, and I just know you'll be hearing from her soon. It will be any day now. Just sit tight if you can. I've talked to her twice, and all I can say is that she seems like a nice person."

"Could I write her — or call her? Could you call her — and see if she has written me?"

"Molly, please understand, I have to try and protect the feelings of everyone involved, and I don't want to harass her in any way. Believe me — she'll contact you. Okay?"

"I guess so. Thanks — I'm sorry if I seem to be such a nuisance."

"Don't worry about it. I've been there before — just try and be patient, but let me know as soon as you hear."

"Patience — that's supposed to be an Asian virtue. Except I wasn't raised by Asians, and I don't think there's such a thing as a patience gene."

Mary laughed. "Just hang in there."

"Okay, I'll try."

As soon as Molly got off the phone with Mary she heard her mother downstairs.

"Hi!" Ellie called up the stairs. "Molly — I'm home."

Molly came down from her room and hugged her mother. "You look tired — bad day?"

"Crummy. Did you hear today?"

"No, Mom. There's nothing. I called Mary, but she said I shouldn't worry. The mail's on the counter." Molly got an apple from the refrigerator and sat at the kitchen table. Her mother put her briefcase down and opened the refrigerator, right after Molly had closed it. She surveyed its contents and then shut the door.

"You know, I bought stuff for dinner but I don't feel much like cooking tonight; maybe we can go out for a bite. It's such a lovely day. We could go down to Pioneer Square and eat at al Boccalino."

"Good idea. When's Dad getting home?"

Ellie looked at her watch. "He should be home pretty soon. He said he'd be home early tonight." She got the newspaper and leafed through the mail that Molly had put on the table.

"Molly? Did you see these?"

"What?"

Her mother held up two small pink slips. "Molly, these are from the post office — they're notices of registered letters!"

She jumped up and looked at the slips. "What? I thought they were just slips about packages or something — you know, some of Dad's stuff." Her dad was always ordering things from the L.L. Bean catalog, and they often got notices of packages to pick up at the post office.

"Molly! This is it — they're from Canada!"

"Oh, Mom!" Molly hugged her mother.

She looked at her watch. "The post office closes in a half hour. We can make it!"

Molly stared at Ellie; she felt suddenly fearful and confused. "Mom — I — "

Ellie put her arm around her. "Come on, honey. Let's go. It'll be all right."

They drove to the post office in the university district in record time. Ellie made every light, but then couldn't find a parking spot. "Molly — I'm going to park right here in front in this bus zone and if we get a ticket — the hell with it!"

They jumped out of the car, and Molly grabbed her mother's hand as they ran up the steps to the post office.

"Sign here." The clerk took the slips and handed them each another form for their signature.

Molly looked at her mother with tears in her eyes as they each signed the forms. The clerk handed them the letters; one addressed to Molly Jane Fletcher and the other addressed to Ellie and Paul Fletcher. They held the letters and stood looking at each other.

"Well," Ellie said, "I guess this is it."

"I love you, Mom," Molly said. She reached for her mother's hand, and they walked out of the post office, clutching their letters, holding hands.

"The car's still here — "

"And no ticket!" Molly said, seeing nothing on the windshield.

"Do you want to read it in the car — or shall we go somewhere, or what — what would you like?"

"Well, we'd better move the car in case a bus comes."

"Right. Yes, that's a good idea," Ellie said. "I know — let's go to the Laurelhurst playfield."

They rode in silence down the big hill, and when they got to Five Corners, Molly said, "Let's stop and get a Baskin-Robbins."

"Why not?" Ellie pulled into the small lot in front of the ice cream store. It had been something of a ritual when Molly was a little girl. They'd get ice cream and then go to the park, and Molly would swing on the swings.

"I'll have French vanilla," Molly said.

"Make that two," Ellie said. They always had loved the same flavors.

At the Laurelhurst playfield, they parked the car and headed for the swings, holding their letters and licking the cones.

They each sat on a swing. Ellie in her linen suit and spectator pumps, and Molly in her white shorts and green T-shirt. Their eyes met, and then they each opened their letters.

Dear Molly,

I have tried to write so many times — I keep starting this letter over and over, and then I cross things out and start again. I don't know where to begin except to tell you that when I signed the papers after you were born, which relinquished my rights as your mother, I thought you had disappeared from my life forever. It was the hardest decision I ever made in my life. I was eighteen. You have always been in my heart and in my thoughts, and when Mary Robinson called and said you were well and wanted to contact me, I felt as though I had been given a precious gift.

As Mary told you, I am a Canadian. My maiden name is Karen Kumai. I am a third-generation Japanese Canadian, or sansei,

226

which is the Japanese term. My grandparents, your great-grandparents, came to Canada in 1927. I was born in Vancouver, British Columbia, and I lived there most of my life. I went to college at the University of British Columbia. I met my husband there. Mike Matsuda and I have been married for twelve years and we have a ten-year-old son. His name is Robert Tameichi Matsuda. We call him Robbie, and he is your half brother.

I know you must want to know about your father. He was a boy I was in love with my freshman year in college. He was an exchange student from Japan. On my side of the family, you are the fourth generation to be born in North America, and the term for your generation is yonsei. The boy's name was Michiyo Mori; he was nineteen when you were born. I would like to tell you more about him, and I'd rather talk with you when we meet. In my own mind, I always had named you — the name was Julie.

I don't know how to describe myself very well. In addition to being a wife and a mother, I am an artist. I majored in fine arts at UBC where I got a master's degree, and my paintings are at the Smythe-Hardwick Gallery in Vancouver and also at a few smaller galleries there, the Yarborough Gallery in Toronto and the Henri Beaumont Gallery in Montreal. The paintings have been selling rather well recently, but it has been quite a struggle for many years. My early work was quite political, and the themes dealt with the internment of Japanese North Americans in the States and in Canada. My mother and her family were in a camp in Alberta when she was between the ages of twelve and fifteen. My husband, Mike, is ten years older than I am. He was an assistant professor in the Engineering Department at UBC when I met him. He left the university five years ago to work for Canaco Oil in Vancouver, and we were transferred to Halifax six months ago. There is currently some oil drilling going on up here, and Mike is involved with the project. I was an only child — I know I'm jumping around here — but I'm just writing everything I can think of as it comes. My father worked on the Canadian ferries, and he was killed in a freak accident when I was seven. My mother never remarried. Other than my art, most of my interests centre around my family. I'm involved in things at Robbie's school. He is quite a hockey player, and our family enjoys sport.

Mary tells me that your parents have been very much involved with you in your decision to try and find me. They must be wonderful people. Words can't express the gratitude I feel toward them. I hope we can have a reunion soon. Please let me know when we can meet.

I feel a sense of urgency for all our sakes, because I feel that now that I have been given this opportunity to have a reunion with you, I don't want to lose any precious moments.

I would love to see a picture of you and your family, Molly, and if you'd like I will send you some pictures of me and my family.

I would like to fly to Vancouver, B.C., as soon as school is out for Robbie, which is next week. We could meet in Vancouver or in Seattle — just let me know what you and your parents would like, and I will be there. I can't wait to hear from you. God bless you for having the courage to search for me.

> *Your friend,*
> *Karen*

As Molly was reading her letter, Ellie read hers. It was shorter, and after she read it she waited for Molly to finish reading.

Dear Ellie and Paul,

When I was in the hospital when the baby was born, the social worker who was handling my case brought me some flowers. She said they were from the couple who was adopting my baby. I knew you must have been kind people to have thought of me. Thank you for the flowers. Thank you from the bottom of my heart for being the mother and father of my baby.

Sincerely,
Karen Matsuda

Molly put her letter down and turned to her mother. Ellie held out her arms to her daughter, and Molly clung to her as Ellie rocked her gently on the swing. Molly cried in her arms.

"She's a good lady, Molly," her mother whispered.

"I know, Mom — and Mom — I have a brother!" Molly laughed and cried all at once. " — and Mom — I'm a fourth-generation Japanese American!"

"Oh, Molly . . ."

"You understand, don't you, Mom?"

Ellie held her daughter and stroked her hair. "Yes, Molly . . . I understand."

Nineteen

Molly's father stuck his head in the kitchen door. "I'm home, you two." Molly and her mother were sitting at the kitchen table, talking intently, and didn't hear him come in at first.

"Oh, Dad" — Molly jumped up and hugged him — "we heard! I got a letter from her — and you and Mom did, too!"

"I know, honey. Mom called." Paul took off his sport coat and joined them at the table. "I rushed home as soon as I could."

"Did she tell you?"

"I wanted you to be the one" — Ellie smiled at Molly — "and Dad didn't want to talk on the phone."

"I'm Japanese — fouth-generation Japanese American!"

"Well, how 'bout that." He shook his head, trying

231

to get it to sink in. "How 'bout that," he kept repeating.

"And I have a half brother. I just can't get over it," she said excitedly.

"For heaven's sake."

"Which one do you want to read first?" Ellie asked. "They're both wonderful."

"Well, I guess the one that's to me, too." He smiled. "This is really something, isn't it?" He took his reading glasses out of his shirt pocket.

Molly and her mother were quiet as they watched him read. He read the letter over, several times. Then finally, he put it down and reached out and held both their hands.

"She's a good lady," he said quietly, his voice cracking. "For heaven's sake, isn't this something?" Her father muttered, staring at Molly. He seemed overwhelmed and didn't speak for a while. Finally he turned to Ellie. "Just reading about the flowers, it all came back to me. You know, I remember calling Crissey's and ordering them as if it had just happened — it had been your idea, Ellie." He took out his handkerchief and blew his nose. "Little Molly Jane. I'll never forget the first moment I held you. What a miracle, just a tiny perfect creature. You had such a shank of black hair — I couldn't get over it. They told us your mother had been discharged the day before — my God — what must it have been like for her to leave there without you?"

"You know, while we were waiting to hear from

her I was getting worried that she might get cold feet. It certainly wasn't inconceivable to me that a person might change her mind about something of this magnitude. And I got angry at the thought of possibly having the rug pulled out after everything we've been through." Ellie sighed. "I'm embarrassed that I wasn't even thinking of what she'd been through."

"Here, Dad" — Molly got her letter — "here, read this one now."

After Paul had finished Karen's letter to Molly, he set it down on the table and took off his reading glasses. "I'm so struck that — well, it's not 'birth-mother,' anymore. She's a person with a whole history and a family tree — this sounds foolish I know, but I don't know what I expected. She didn't say much about your father, did she?"

Molly's eyes met his. "You're my father."

Paul's eyes filled with tears.

"I guess she just wants to tell me about my birthfather when we meet," Molly added softly.

"When do you think we should have the reunion?" Ellie wondered. "We might as well decide now because, Molly, you should probably discuss that in your letter to her. Dad and I will want to write her a note, too."

Molly got the calendar that was hanging on the wall next to the phone. "There's the Tolo next weekend — I'd love a great reason like this to get out of it."

"That wouldn't be very nice to the boy," Paul said.

"I know. I know — just a thought. I must always be nice."

"Do you think the next weekend after that is too soon?" Molly pointed to the first weekend in June on the calendar. "She said her son would be out of school next week — they must get out pretty early up there."

"I think we should go as soon as we can," her father said.

"Paul, that's how I felt, but I didn't know you would, too."

"This is quite something for everyone — and I think we should just move ahead."

"Where should we meet?" Molly wondered. "Mary Robinson and her family met in the N.A.S.O. office — but I don't really want to meet there, do you?"

Ellie shook her head. "I don't want to meet in the office, either."

"I don't either. Do you want to invite her to come here?" Paul asked.

"I think it should be more halfway. Listen, I've got an idea — " Ellie was excited. "You know Karen said they would be willing to fly to Vancouver — why don't we drive up to Blaine and meet at the border park at the U.S.–Canadian border? The park is lovely there, and we could have a picnic and spend most of the day."

"Mom, I love that idea."

"So do I," Paul agreed. "I suppose if it rains we

could just drive to Blaine and eat at a restaurant or something."

"Sure, or we could eat under umbrellas." Ellie laughed.

"Or a tent!" Molly said.

They looked at the calendar and settled on the date. "Well, I guess I can write her now and tell her when we want to meet. I know what she meant about it being hard to write. It's kind of strange, I mean — I don't exactly know what to say."

"Why don't you work on your letter some more while Dad and I go out to dinner."

After her parents left, Molly went up to her room and curled up on her bed with a large pad of notebook paper. She reached for Karen's letter to her and reread it several times. Then she stared some more at the blank page. And then looked out the window.

I'm not making much progress here, she thought. This is stupid. At this rate this letter will never get written. Molly forced herself to start writing, but after one sentence she crumpled up the page and threw it on the floor. Three more tries ended up the same way.

She's not going to decide not to come if the letter's not so hot, Molly thought. This isn't a term paper. There won't be a grade. You don't flunk Letter Writing to Birthmothers, so just go ahead and write something. The hell with it. Write anything.

235

Finally she talked herself into it and plunged ahead.

Dear Karen,

I've started this letter what seems like a million times, and I know what you mean about how hard it is to know what to say. I can only tell you how glad I am that we can meet. I've wondered about you my whole life. I understand what you mean about having the reunion right away; part of the reason I wanted to go ahead was that I was afraid something could have happened to you.

My mom and dad are wonderful, and even though it was hard for them at first when I decided I wanted to try and find you — they've really been there for me.

The people with N.A.S.O. have been just great, too, and Mary Robinson is an adoptee herself so she was a big help.

I was so afraid I might never find you or that you wouldn't want to have anything to do with me. I can't tell you how much it means to me to know who you are. Mary Robinson said sometimes birthmothers refuse — I was so afraid of that.

I will be graduating from high school the third week in June. Usually, graduation is a lot earlier than that — but there was a teacher's strike in Seattle last fall, and school got started late. In the fall I'll be a freshman at Whitman College in Walla Walla, Washington. It's a strange name for a town, but the college is a good small liberal arts school. There are some famous onions that are grown in Walla Walla — that's about all it's known for. (I can't believe I'm writing you about onions.) I don't know what to tell you about me. I know we'll have a lot of time to talk. Dad is a physiologist; he does research at the Dexter Horton Research Center here in Seattle. Mom is a doctor, she's a pediatrician. We belong to the University Unitarian Church.

I have been active in student council, and I was a cheerleader this year. (This letter is starting to sound so dumb to me — oh, well.) I'm not sure what I want to major in, in college, but I'm thinking about education. I think I'd like to be a teacher. I really love little kids, and I loved learning about Robbie — I really can't believe I have a little brother!

We'd like to meet you the first weekend in June on the 3rd. Is that a good time for you? Mom wondered if you'd like to meet us for an all-day picnic at the border park near the U.S.– Canadian border. There is a beautiful monument there, the Peace Arch. It's not too far south of Vancouver. Let me know if this is okay with you and your family. I've enclosed my senior picture and a snapshot of me with my mom and dad. Please send me a picture of you and Mike and Robbie.

When I come to meet you I'm going to bring all our family albums so you can see how I looked and grew up all these past eighteen years. I'd like to know all about my background and would love to see any family albums you have. I also would like to have medical records or maybe you could just tell me about the medical history of your family.

Thank you for telling me about my birth-father. I like it that I'm a yonsei. My closest guy friend, Roland Hirada, is Japanese, too. Well, he used to be my closest friend — it's kind of a complicated situation. It's too involved to get into, but I can't tell you what it means to know what I am.

I can't wait to meet you!

Your friend,
Molly

After Molly finished the letter she reread it and felt it was completely inadequate. But it was the best she could do, and she knew she'd have to send it.

When she finished addressing the letter, she reached for the phone and called Roland's number and then hung up before it started ringing. Damn. She missed him so much. They had hardly spoken since that time when he made her so mad and she hung up on him. *Why did everything have to get screwed up?*

On Tuesday of the following week when Molly got home she checked the mail and found another letter from Karen, Express Mail. The June 3rd date was fine with them, and they had already made their plane reservations. Enclosed in the letter was a snapshot of Karen with Mike and Robbie. The three of them had their arms around each other with the little boy in the middle. It looked like it had been taken in a park. In the background there was a lake with ducks on it. The parents were wearing jeans and sweatshirts, but the little boy looked like he had on some kind of a sports uniform shirt with a number 99 on it. Like a Seahawks shirt or something, but of course it wouldn't be the Seahawks. Probably some Canadian team.

Molly stared at the picture for what seemed like hours. "We look kind of alike," she thought, as she stared at the woman's face in the photograph. *"I look like someone!"* she shouted and then laughed, catching herself shouting in the empty house. She looked at the boy. What a darling little guy. Robbie. My brother. *That's my little brother.*

She noticed that Karen's eyes were large and wide-set with the brows shaped just like hers, but Karen's face was narrower and more oval-shaped. Molly wondered if Karen would have a picture of her birthfather that she would bring. I must have gotten my high cheekbones from him, she thought. The man in the picture — Robbie's father — he looked nice, handsome, too. What a nice-looking family. They all matched — all Asian.

Suddenly she felt exhausted and, taking the picture, she went up to her room and lay down on her bed. She wished her parents were home so she could show them the picture. She wanted to be with them . . . with her own family. Molly propped the picture against the lamp next to her bed, and lay on her side staring at it. Within minutes, she was sound asleep. She slept until the next morning.

At breakfast she showed the picture to her parents.

"What a beautiful family." Ellie stared at it then handed it to Paul. But she didn't seem to share Molly's excitement.

"Are you okay, Mom?"

"I guess I was just feeling a little sad. I was wishing, well — just that we could have given you a little brother."

"Oh, Mom — " Molly didn't know what to say.

Her father looked at it a long time before giving it back to her. "Molly, if we'd known you were Japanese I wonder if we would have done something. I mean, insisted that you study Japanese in school, wanted you to learn about the culture you came from."

"You guys are being silly." She laughed. "Roland's

fourth-generation Japanese American and the only Japanese words he knows are Sony, Honda, Mitsubishi, Toyota, Ramen, karate and *sayonara*."

Paul and Ellie looked at each other and laughed. "Well, I've got to get to the office." Her father pushed his chair back from the table. "Say, how is Roland? He doesn't seem to come around here much anymore."

"No," Molly said flatly. "He doesn't."

Twenty

It was raining the night of the Tolo. It had started shortly before noon when the sky had clouded over and the slow drizzle began misting the brilliant green of the Seattle spring morning with its persistent dampening gray.

In the afternoon, Molly and Kathy had gotten their hair done together at the Gene Juarez Salon at Nordstrom's. Afterwards, they cruised all the cosmetic counters and found one that was giving free makeovers. "Let's go for it," Kathy said, hopping onto the stool in front of the Elizabeth Arden counter and pulling Molly up on the one next to her.

The saleslady convinced them that there were quite a number of products that they couldn't live without, and they left the store forty-five minutes later with considerably more makeup on their faces and less money in their pockets.

On the way home when Kathy stopped at a red

light, Molly pulled down the visor on the passenger's side and looked in the mirror, scowling at her reflection. "I think I look like I'm about to go to work on Pike Street for the evening."

"Hardly. Trust me — you look great."

Now as she looked at herself in the bathroom mirror, she thought the whole thing was really a bit much. Kathy had helped her pick out the dress; it had an emerald-green strapless top that was tightly fitted, accentuating her small waist, a good feature that made her top look bigger, Kathy had pointed out. At the hips, the skirt, which was the same emerald satin but covered with tiny black polka dots, flared slightly, the hem hitting right above the knee.

Molly went to the full-length mirror in her parents' room to check the whole thing out. At least the thunder thighs are pretty well covered, she thought, but this thing sure is short. Maybe she shouldn't have gotten such high heels. Kathy said they *made* the dress, the heels and the black sheer stockings with the tiny black dots — but she felt like a little kid clomping around in her mother's shoes. It wasn't as if she hadn't worn heels often enough before, but these things were like walking around on stilts.

Molly turned on the TV and some of the lights in her parents' bedroom. Of all weekends, she wished this hadn't been the one of those pediatric meetings at Rosario's on Orcas Island that they went to every year. She turned the volume up on the TV a little bit more, wanting to make sure Joe would think they were home. There was a time when she probably would have felt uneasy about the whole charade, but she realized that she didn't worry about being quite that nice anymore. If it helped handle Joe to have him think her parents were around, fine.

Walking back down the hall to her room, she went in her bathroom and fooled around with her hair some more. She missed her parents. She wanted someone to tell her she looked okay. Maybe this whole outfit really was too flashy, she thought, needing more reassurance. Then she tried to remind herself that when she had tried the dress on for them that morning they both said she was stunning. Dad got kind of shook up, too. All that my-little-girl-is-all-grown-up stuff.

The minute she heard the doorbell, Molly began to perspire. Oh, great, now I turn into a complete pit before I even get to the dance. She grabbed her deodorant as the bell rang again. This is ridiculous. She put the deodorant back and went down the stairs.

"Some dress, Fletcher." Joe smiled appreciatively as she opened the door.

"Thanks. But to tell you the truth, I wish we were having those same old Hawaiian Tolos so we could just wear shorts." Molly looked out across the yard. "It's still really coming down, huh?"

"I don't have an umbrella — do you want to bring one?"

"No — I'll just put my coat over my head."

"Are you all set?"

"Yeah — oh, my parents said to say 'hi' — they're upstairs getting ready to go out."

"Are they going to be back late?"

"No — very early."

Molly put her coat over her head as they ran for the car. The minute Joe asked how late they'd be she could just see his mind work. Did he ever think about anything but sex? He was one guy you would not want to have know you were alone in the house. She was glad she had given him that line of bull.

In the car Molly had trouble buckling the seat belt.

"That sticks sometimes — let me do it." He leaned over, snapped the buckle in place, and then slipped his arm across her waist and started to kiss her.

"Gimme a break, Joe." Molly pulled back, leaning toward the door. "I spent a fortune getting my hair done and on all this stupid makeup. I don't want to get all messed up before we even get there."

Joe laughed as he backed out of the drive. "You could never look messed up, Fletcher. You look great with makeup or without. With or without — " He eyed her dress.

When they got to the school Joe drove to the door nearest the gym. "Listen, since it's raining, I'll drop you off here. I'll meet you inside after I find a parking space."

"I'll be at the table where they take the tickets."

"Okay. I shouldn't be too long."

As Molly walked down the hall toward the gym, she could hear the beat of the reggae music pounding through the building. She checked her coat on the rack behind the table where the chaperones were sitting and hung around the ticket table while she waited for Joe. She looked into the gym. It was a great crowd. Kathy was dancing right in the middle of the floor, wilder than anyone, as usual. She waved and gave Molly a big thumbs up as soon as she saw her.

All week at school Molly had been aware of how she had found herself noticing the Asian kids in a way she hadn't before — not just the Asian kids, but specifically the Japanese kids. She had that same awareness tonight as she watched people on the dance floor. Eric Mizuki, Beth Hara, Rachel Maneki were a few that she noticed right away — it was amazing how conscious she was of them.

She was starting to feel stupid, standing there by herself, and looked down the hall for Joe. She saw a lot of couples coming toward the door, but still no sign of him. Then she saw Roland. He had on a dark suit, and for a minute she wasn't sure if it was even him. But there was no mistaking Megan. Molly's stomach turned over when she saw them together. She spun around and walked along the coatracks as fast as she could. Fumbling in the pocket of her coat as if she had forgotten something, she pretended she hadn't seen them. Where was

Joe, anyway? It couldn't be that hard to find a parking space. Out of the corner of her eye she saw Megan and Roland go into the gym. Megan looked like her dress would fall off at any moment.

In a few minutes Joe came down the hall toward the ticket table. He put his arm around her, leaned down and whispered in her ear. "Wanna do it?"

"What's with you, Joe?"

He threw back his head and laughed. "Dance! Wanna dance?" As he hovered next to her, she smelled beer on his breath.

"Got started early, huh?"

"Just a quick one in the parking lot. I've got a couple of six packs out there. We can go out whenever we want."

The music was fast, and Molly had to admit he was a great dancer. The guy was sexy. No getting around it. And he loved the attention — moving his hips like Michael Jackson on that old video — *Bad*. Everyone checked him out. Especially the girls.

"We've got the house from eleven to twelve, Fletcher."

"I can't hear you!" Molly danced closer to him. "It's so loud — "

He reached out and grabbed her and pulled her to him while he kept dancing, moving his hips, holding her against him. "We've got the house — from eleven to twelve. Brad Sorenson's parents are out of town. Some of us are using the house on shifts. We've got eleven to twelve."

"I love this song." Molly put her hands on his shoulders and gave him a shove. "I wanna dance, Joe."

The song ended, and Joe loosened his tie and opened his collar. "Man, it's hot." Sweat poured off his forehead, and he took off his jacket and slung it over his shoulder. "I'm ready for a cold one."

"So soon?"

"Sure — why not?"

"You just had one."

"Come on out with me."

"You just got here, Joe."

"Believe me, I'll know when it's eleven. Sure you don't want to come out with me now?"

"Go ahead — I don't feel like it."

"Okay. Catch you later."

Molly walked across the gym toward the girls' locker room. Maybe she'd just disappear in there for a while. She wished she had known what to say when Joe told her they had this shift at Sorenson's house. It upset her. All those guys getting together and figuring out when they'd each have an appointment to screw. Real romantic. Did he actually think that was a turn on? She might as well be on an assembly line. She wove her way through the crowd, wishing she were anywhere but at this stupid dance.

"Molly?"

"What?" Molly squinted. It was hard to see in the dark gym. She moved closer to the door. Then her eyes met his. Roland was leaning back against the wall, with his hands in his pockets. Her voice caught in her throat. "Hi."

"You look so beautiful. I hardly recognized you at first."

"Oh, thanks a lot. I looked like a real dog before, huh?"

"That's not what I meant, Molly," he said quietly.

"Where's Megan?"

"She and Rachel Maneki went into the bathroom to have a cigarette."

"Oh."

"They've been gone awhile, though. I think they went up on the third floor. Rachel has some pot. Where's Joe?"

"Out in the car having a beer."

"He starts early, huh?"

"I guess so."

"Dire Straights." Roland smiled, pointing toward the D.J. who had just put on one of their slow songs. He and Molly had agreed once a long time ago that it was their all-time favorite band. Roland looked down at her. "Dance?"

"What if Megan comes back?" she said coldly.

"What if Joe comes back?" he shot back.

"Oh, okay."

They walked out on the floor, not touching. She tried to appear nonchalant, but inside she felt like a quivering mass of nerves. Slowly he slipped his hand around her waist and took her hand. He held her away from him, just looking at her.

"Great song." She tried to sound casual. Then looking up at him, she found herself staring, taking in his strong face, his gentle dark eyes. What was different about him? It couldn't just be the suit. It was just Roland — but had he always been this handsome?

He held her carefully, cautiously, as though she might break in his arms.

"I've missed you, Molly."

A lump caught in her throat. It took her by surprise, and she didn't know what to say.

"How've you been?"

"Oh, Roland — so much has happened." She felt like a dam was about to burst.

"Let's get out of here."

"We can't — "

"Screw them."

"Do you mean that? What about Megan?"

"She's nothing to me. I don't know why you never could believe that. Are you worried about Joe?"

"I can't stand him," she said quietly.

"Okay, so we're leaving."

"But how can we just leave? It wouldn't be very nice to just dump them like that."

"I thought you didn't want to be so nice anymore?"

"Well — "

"They're both just getting high, anyway. Molly — I need to be with you."

"I have so much to tell you — "

'Come on. We're outta here."

"We have to tell them something."

"Okay. We'll get sick — "

"What?"

"You know — tell them we're sick. That we have to go home."

"Oh, Roland." Molly eyes sparkled. "You're too much."

"Do you want to say you have a terrible headache or do you want to say you're going to throw up?"

"I'll be about to throw up, and you can get the headache."

"I'll meet you at your house in a half hour."

Molly changed into her jeans and sweatshirt. It hadn't been as hard to get Joe to take her home as she thought. Once he thought she might throw up all over him he seemed quite content to leave the dance, and there hadn't been any big wrestling match in the car in her driveway, either. What a relief. She knew he was the kind of guy who was sure he'd have no trouble finding someone else for his lousy eleven-to-twelve shift. And the disgusting thing was, he was probably right.

As soon as she got home she gathered up the picture of Karen, Mike, and Robbie, and Karen's letters and took them down to the living room and put them on the coffee table in front of the couch. There was so much to tell him. She knew she had missed Roland, but she hadn't realized how terribly

251

much. What a hole there had been in her life without him. Upstairs she brushed her hair, waiting for him to come and then flew down the stairs the minute she heard the doorbell.

"Molly — " He closed the door behind him and took her in his arms, almost lifting her off the ground. "Oh, baby — I've missed you so much."

She clung to him with her arms tight around his neck, not wanting to let go. "Roland — I — "

"Shhh — " He held her to him, his face pressed against her hair.

She took his hand and led him to the living room and pulled him down on the couch next to her. "Roland — I found her."

"Your birthmother?"

Molly nodded.

"Oh, Molly — "

"And guess what?" she whispered.

"Tell me."

"I'm Japanese — a *yonsei*."

Roland grinned. "For God's sakes — that's what I am. Fourth generation, right?"

"Absolutely." Molly reached for the picture on the table.

"I can't believe this."

"Look. I just got this in the mail last week."

He stared at the picture. "Your birthmother — "

"Yes."

"And that little guy?"

"My brother. I have a half brother — can you

imagine? His name is Robbie. Robbie Matsuda."

"She's so pretty. She's really young-looking — "

"She's thirty-six. Do you think we look alike?"

"Your faces are shaped a little differently. I always thought you looked like Linda Tiara on CNN."

"You never told me that before."

"I never told me a lot of things before."

"But you do think I look like her — like Karen?"

"Yes. Especially your eyes — you and the little boy look a lot alike, too."

"I know this must sound dumb. But it means everything in the world to me to know there's someone I look like."

Roland put the photograph back on the table and put his arm around her. "It's not dumb."

They talked until three in the morning. He read Karen's letters, and Molly went over every detail of what had happened since Mary Robinson had first called her with the news that she had located Karen. "I wanted to call you so many times." Molly looked sad for a moment. "Sometimes I did — I'd just call and let it ring. Then I'd hang up."

Roland was quiet. "How did we get so far apart?"

"I hated seeing you with Megan. I couldn't handle any of it."

"Look — she was exciting for a while. I admit it. But she's not in your league. There's just nothing to her, Molly."

"Promise?"

"Of course — but what about Joe?"

"He's a jerk."

"I told you so."

"Don't say it, Roland. I don't want to get back into it. All that stupid arguing."

"We won't. I won't let it."

"Are you hungry?"

"Possibly." He laughed.

"Come on." She grabbed his hand and pulled him up from the couch. In the kitchen they decided to make bacon and scrambled eggs.

"Roland" — Molly turned the heat down and flipped the bacon over — "all we've done is talk about me."

"Believe me, the things in my life are mild. Not like what you've been going through."

"I heard you got a scholarship to Seattle U."

"Who told you?"

"Kathy, I guess. Congratulations — that's so great!"

"It's the year of the little man. Who knows, someday I may join the ranks of the all-pro 5'9"-and-under jocks. There's Spud Webb of the Atlanta Hawks, Frank Minnifield of the Cleveland Browns, Lionel 'Little Train' James of the San Diego Chargers, Joe Morris of the New York Giants and his brother, Jamie Morris, of the Washington Redskins — "

"And soon after a great career at Seattle U. in football and basketball — Roland Hirada of the Seattle Seahawks or even the Sonics!" Molly tore off some sheets of paper towel and lifted the bacon onto them to drain.

"It's fun to think about. Anyway — I hear you're going to Whitman."

"Kathy told you that, too?" She smiled. "Kath' must have been quite the pipeline during all this." Molly lifted the kitchen window to let out the smoke from the bacon, which had burned a little. Then she opened the refrigerator.

"Did she tell you this?" He closed the refrigerator door, turned her toward him and held her face in his hands. "Did she tell you that I love you?"

"Roland — "

His lips brushed hers, and then he pulled her against him, and his gentle kiss became eager and insistent. Cool air filled the room from the open kitchen window and outside the wind swept across the midnight blue of the lake, churning its smooth surface, and the pine boughs shuddered in the late-night air. Molly felt his body press into hers, and her heart beat against his warm chest like the wings of a young bird. "Oh, Roland — " She opened her eyes slowly, feeling the sting of tears and the pain of too much tenderness. "I've missed you so much."

"Molly — "

"I love you," she said softly. "I always have — I just didn't know it."

Twenty-One

"Did I wake you up?" Molly whispered into the phone, not wanting to disturb her parents.

"No — it only rang once." Roland yawned. "Justin can sleep through an earthquake. Are you okay?"

"I hardly slept."

"Are you nervous or excited?"

"Both — scared, everything. I can't believe we're leaving this morning."

"I wish I could be with you."

"So do I."

"How long does it take to get up there?"

"I think Blaine is just a couple of hours. Roland, I'm really scared."

"She seems like a nice lady. It'll all be okay."

"I'm worried about Mom and Dad."

"How are they doing?"

"They seem okay, but now that it's really here the

old fears are all back bugging me. I think they are for Mom, too. She hasn't said anything, but I can just tell. Roland, I couldn't stand it if this hurt them. We've been over it together a million times, but it's making me crazy — I wish I could get my mind off it, even for a minute."

"Let's see, how 'bout if I sing you my latest song?"

"I thought you guys missed the deadline for that MTV contest."

"We did. But that didn't finish Rockin' Roland's career as a songwriter. Listen to this one." Roland cleared his throat, then sang out into the phone, *"You treat me like garbage. . . . You treat me like trash. . . . You put me down the drain like old corned beef hash. . . . I'm just the garbage man of lo-ove . . . Dump-ster Dump-ster Dump-ster man."*

Molly covered the mouthpiece trying to muffle her laughter.

"Molly? Are you speechless? Great song, isn't it?"

"I am Roland. I am truly speechless." Molly laughed, then she looked at the clock next to her bed. "Oh, it's eight already — I guess I'd better get up and get dressed."

"Molly?"

"Hmmm?"

"When we go to the prom, wear that green dress."

"I love you."

"Me, too. I'm sure it will be okay, Mol. Call me as soon as you get back."

Molly put on her favorite pair of jeans and a polo

shirt that she had laid out the night before. After she was dressed she sat on her bed, staring at Karen's picture. She decided to call Mary Robinson.

After a few rings Mary answered the phone in a sleepy voice.

"Mary — it's Molly — I know it's early but — "

"Oh, don't worry," she said, beginning to sound more alert. "It's the big day, isn't it?"

"Yes, and I'm so uptight — I'm really excited — but scared, too. I still can't believe this is happening."

"I've been involved as a C.I. in a number of reunions, and from what I know of your family and of Karen, I think this is one of the especially nice ones. There are lots of good ones — but some are terribly painful and disappointing."

"Like that guy at the meeting whose birthmother turned out to be the biker — "

"That was one of them. . . ."

"Mary, what if she doesn't like me?"

"Right now she's probably worrying that you will have trouble accepting her because she gave you up in the first place. The birthmothers have a lot of guilt to contend with."

"I understand — I mean, I know she didn't want to — that she just couldn't take care of me."

"Then tell her."

"Mary?"

"Yes?"

"Thank you for finding her."

"Of course . . . call me as soon as you get back and Molly, don't worry. It will be all right."

At the Halifax airport, Mike waited at the Air Canada gate with Karen and Robbie for their flight to Vancouver. They were only taking carry-on luggage, and Karen absentmindedly played with the handle of her small suitcase, which she had filled with family photo albums, medical records and the few clothes she would need for the weekend. Robbie sat between his parents holding his backpack on his lap, with the Clayton Park Bluenosers hocky team pictures in it, his Great Gretzky Yearbook and a present for Molly. "I wish you could come with us, Dad."

"I thought I explained that — I can't leave the drilling right now, Rob."

The ticket agent announced that flight 399 for Vancouver would begin boarding in twenty minutes.

"Is that us, Mom?"

"That's us."

"Do I have time to get some candy?"

Karen looked down the corridor at the newsstand. "Okay — but hurry right back." She opened her purse and took a dollar from her wallet. "Here."

"And some gum, too?"

"Sure, but come right back."

She took the tickets from her purse, checking their boarding passes as Robbie ran off toward the newsstand.

259

Mike reached for a newspaper that had been left on the seat next to him and turned to the sports page. He and Karen had developed an uneasy truce, but the impending reunion lay between them like some unnavigable body of water. He put down the paper. "Are you even going to call Yuri when you get there?"

Karen didn't answer him right away. She had decided to stay at a hotel and then rent a car Saturday morning to drive to Blaine. Her mother's anger at her decision hadn't changed, and the last thing she wanted was to spend the night before the reunion at her mother's house. The whole thing was hard enough as it was without having to put up with her icy disapproval. "Yes, I'll call her," she said, quietly. "For Robbie's sake. But I don't have a whole lot to say to her."

"Or to me — "

"Look, Mike — I love you. You're my husband, and I just hope when this whole thing is over you'll be able to get that through your head." She looked toward the newsstand and saw Robbie come running toward them. "If you only could have come with us — "

"I'm here."

"I know — but — "

"Listen, Karen. I'm here seeing you off. Maybe this is just the best I can do right now."

She stood up as their flight was called and mo-

260

tioned for Robbie, who came bounding up to them. "Now, Mom?"

"Come on, honey. We've got to get on the plane."

Mike hugged Robbie and then looked at Karen. "I'll see you Monday."

She put her suitcase down and put her arms around him. "Thanks for taking us to the airport." She held him tightly. "Please understand — " she whispered and then turned and headed to the boarding gate with Robbie, fighting back tears.

When Karen and Robbie arrived in Vancouver they picked up their rental car at the airport and drove to the Bayshore Inn. "Do you want to have dinner here?" she asked him, as they checked in.

"Yeah. We can eat at McDonald's any old time."

In the hotel coffee shop Robbie devoured a hamburger and chips, drowning the hamburger in catsup and sloshing the chips with so much vinegar that Karen thought the whole mess looked inedible. "I like it this way, Mom — really."

"Well, I guess you're the one eating it, not me."

She picked at her food, hardly eating a thing. "How do you like the hotel, Rob?"

"Cool. I just wish I'd brought a bathing suit."

"I didn't think of it. I'm sorry. The pool looks nice, doesn't it?"

"Yeah. Are we going to get to see Gramma?"

"Let's call her after dinner." Karen took a sip of

her coffee. "See, this trip really isn't to visit her — we'll see her next time."

"She doesn't want to meet my sister, does she?"

"No. It's complicated, Robbie. But Gramma doesn't want to talk to us or to anyone about it."

"I wish we could have brought Betsey to meet Molly."

Karen laughed. "I think we've got enough stuff to show her, don't you think?"

In the elevator on the way up to their room Karen felt queasy. Maybe she should have made herself eat something — just forced herself. She looked down at Robbie. Thank God he was with her. She'd probably feel better after they got the phone call out of the way. Then if she got her appetite back, she could order room service. Robbie'd probably think that would be great.

He turned on the TV as soon as they got in the room.

"Let's wait to watch — I think we should call Gramma before it gets too late. She goes to bed pretty early."

"Okay." He turned it off and sat on the bed next to the phone, waiting while Karen called.

"Mother?"

"Are you in town now?" Yuri's voice was flat and expressionless.

"The plane was a little late. We're at the Bay-shore — we just finished dinner. We leave for Blaine first thing in the morning. How are you feeling?"

"Fine. Have you told Hiroko about any of this?"

"No."

"Karen, what if this girl wants money? What if she wants to contact the Mori family? Have you thought of that?"

"For God's sake, Mother — "

"The Mori family must never know about this!"

"Is that all you can think about?"

"Don't shout at me, Karen!"

"Robbie's right here. He wants to say hello." Karen handed the phone to Robbie and went into the bathroom and shut the door. Damn her. Why had she even bothered to call? She should have known it would just make her feel awful. She turned on the faucet and splashed her face with cold water.

"Mom! Do you want to say good-bye to Gramma?"

"No, Rob — you go ahead. Just say good-bye for me."

In the morning when the desk phoned with their wake-up call, Karen realized she had hardly slept at all, but her appetite had come back a little and at breakfast she was at least able to get down some toast and juice. Robbie had a huge stack of pancakes. After two cups of coffee she was feeling more awake. They checked out of the hotel and were in their rental car by nine heading south to the Canadian-American border.

"Rob — take the map, will you?"

"Okay." He grinned, feeling important as the navigator.

"Just make sure we get on 99." She had known the way out of the city all her life. But somehow it helped to have Robbie checking it out on the map.

"This is 99 here, Mom."

"Okay. Yeah, I see — thanks." She smiled over at him. "Good job."

"I hope she'll like my present," he said, periodically checking his backpack to see if it was all right.

Karen looked at her watch. "We're in good shape. We're supposed to meet them at the park across from the Peace Arch at the border at noon."

"Are we almost there?"

"No. We've got quite a way to go, yet."

That morning Mabel Wiley watched closely as the Fletchers packed their car. Ellie brought out a picnic basket loaded with cold fried chicken, potato salad, fruit and chocolate cake. "Looks like a family picnic," Mabel squeaked from across the hedge. "Going to play some games, I see." She peered into the garage as Paul opened the trunk and put in a soccer ball, a Frisbee, a baseball, mitts and a bat, which he thought would be good to have for whatever Robbie might want to play.

"Very observant, Mabel." Paul took the box from Molly that held every picture that had ever been taken of her and put it in the backseat.

"Where are you off to?"

"A foreign country." He went to the back of the car and shut the trunk.

"Your father's a real card, Molly Jane."

"That's right, Mrs. Wiley."

"Is Ronald going? He certainly has been around a lot again this past week."

"What a surprise that you noticed, Mrs. Wiley." Molly got in the backseat and waved while they pulled out of the driveway.

"You know it has been nice to have him around again," her mother said, as they turned onto 45th. "I missed him."

"So did I." Molly smiled.

"Ah — young love — " Molly's father looked back and winked at her.

"I always knew you two were a lot more than friends."

"Mother's intuition, huh, Mom?"

"Must have been."

Molly curled up on the backseat and closed her eyes.

"Why don't you try to sleep, too," Molly heard her father whisper to her mother. "You didn't get much sleep last night."

"You're right. I just keep worrying."

"Isn't it a bit late for that?"

"About the food. I wonder if I brought enough food."

"Shhh — don't worry. Just close your eyes."

Molly and her mother slept until they got to Bellingham, and Molly spent most of the ride from there to the border combing her hair, while her mother talked incessantly about how there would never be enough chicken to go around, and she was sure the cake would be awful, and that the fruit must have rotted.

"Now calm down, you two — we're here," Paul said gently as they drove into the park. He looked at his watch. "It's ten of twelve — pretty good timing."

They got out of the car and looked anxiously around.

Her parents began unpacking the trunk, but Molly stood frozen.

"Mom . . . what if they don't come?"

Ellie put her arms around her daughter. "Don't worry, honey. We're a few minutes early."

"Sometimes there's a backup on the Canadian side," her father said. "On Saturday mornings a lot of Vancouver people come over here to shop."

Her father put his arm around her. "It's going to be all right."

"What if she — ?"

"Now here — take this baseball mitt; we can play catch while we wait. Roland thinks you're a pretty good catch."

Molly gave him a tense smile, and they walked over to a grassy spot while Ellie set the food out on the picnic table.

* * *

Karen and Robbie had only a short wait at the border, and Karen was relieved as she saw the Peace Arch looming before them. The park was on the left side, and her heart began pounding as she pulled the rental car into the parking lot.

"Mom, look!" Robbie said, excitedly. "I think I see them! Look — over there!"

They got out of the car, and Karen saw a picnic table where a tall, gray-haired, middle-aged woman was putting food on the table while a man was playing catch with a lovely Asian girl.

"Robbie," Karen whispered, "I know you're too old for this — but — "

"But what, Mom?"

"Hold my hand — okay?"

"Okay." Robbie took his mother's hand. In his other hand he clutched his Great Gretzky Yearbook and his present for Molly.

Molly looked up and dropped the baseball when she saw the woman and the little boy wearing the Edmonton Oilers shirt with the number 99 on it walking toward them.

She looked at Ellie, "Mom — it's them!"

"Molly?" Karen said, fighting back tears.

Molly went to her and looked into Karen's dark eyes and reached out to her. She felt a warm surge go through her as they held each other. She had a peaceful feeling unlike any she had ever known.

When Karen let go of Molly, she looked at Paul and Ellie Fletcher. She couldn't speak.

Ellie Fletcher reached out and hugged Karen. "How can we ever thank you? She is the joy of our lives."

"Hi, Molly," Robbie said timidly.

"Oh, Robbie, can I hug you, too?"

Robbie grinned as Molly bent down and put her arms around his thin shoulders.

"I have a present for you."

"You do?"

"Yep. Wanna see it now, eh?"

"Why don't we go over to the table? Molly has something for you, too, Robbie." Paul Fletcher took out his handerkerchief and blew his nose.

They sat at the picnic table, and Robbie handed Molly a jar wrapped in red-white-and-blue wrapping paper. "I picked the paper 'cause of the colors," he said, grinning.

"Oh, thank you!" She took off the paper and held a jar. It was the size and shape of a mustard jar and the label read, *Bay of Fundy Mud*.

Molly looked puzzled. "Uh — what is it, Robbie?"

"It's mud."

"Mud?" Molly laughed.

"Yep. It's real mud, and it comes from the highest tides in the world 'cause they're in the Bay of Fundy, and that's near Halifax where I live."

"Oh, that's wonderful — I love having this mud!" She laughed. "I'll bet there's no one in all of Seattle who has mud like this." She reached into the picnic

268

basket and brought out a small package. "Here, now this is for you."

Robbie opened the package. In it was a small plastic pouch that looked like it had gray powder in it.

"What's this stuff?"

"It's ash. It's from our volcano when Mt. St. Helens blew up. They sold packages of the ash — real volcanic ash — and I thought you might like something that was especially from Washington."

"Pretty good. Ash and mud." Robbie grinned and then looked around at the food. "When do we eat?"

Laughter, show-and-tell, and tears filled the afternoon. They looked at all the pictures of Molly, and of all of Karen's relatives, until Robbie got bored and played ball with Paul. Karen told Molly and Ellie what she knew of how the Kumai family came to Canada from Japan. "The Asian Exclusion Act had been passed in the States in 1924, and it was easier for people from Japan who wanted to emigrate to get into Canada. They came in 1927. My grandfather started as a laborer and was able to save enough to get a small truck farm outside of Vancouver — but then of course with the war they lost everything."

"Where were they interned?" Ellie asked.

"In Alberta — I guess it was horrible. My mother was twelve at the time. She can't even talk about it, even to this day."

"It was such a shameful chapter in American history — you forget that the Japanese-Canadians went through it, too," Ellie said. "It's very easy for me to get on a soapbox about this. You want to think that it's all in the past, but I remember not that long ago when Senator Inouye was chairing the Senate committee that was investigating the Iran-contra mess, all the hate mail he got — people calling him a foreigner and a Jap. It was despicable!"

"Mom's pretty political." Molly smiled. "Roland's grandfather was in the 442nd with Senator Inouye. I guess I didn't say a lot about him in my letter. But actually a lot happened with him and me since I wrote — "

"His grandfather was in the 442nd? So he's Japanese?"

"Like me — fourth generation. Roland told me once that he thought there was sort of an uptight nerd image about being Japanese-American. Being studious and a grind and all. I used to think he set out deliberately to destroy that idea. He can get outrageous sometimes — but he makes me laugh. The ironic thing, I guess, is that I never even knew what kind of an Asian I was — "

"Molly — I know you want to find out about your birthfather. I just didn't want to put too much in the letter."

"Those letters were so hard to write, anyway."

"Yes, mine took me hours to write — and it was

after several tries, eh?" Karen smiled. "I almost felt like it turned into a résumé."

"When I read mine over, I thought it sounded like I was about twelve!"

Karen was quiet for a moment. Then she reached into her bag. "This is the UBC yearbook from 1969." She opened it to a page where she had put a bookmark and laid it flat on the table. It was a group photograph of exchange students. "This is your birthfather," she said softly, pointing to a handsome young man in the second row. "His name is Michiyo Mori."

Molly and Ellie stared at the picture. No one spoke while Karen looked across the park where Molly's father and Robbie were throwing the Frisbee.

"There's quite a resemblance." Ellie put her hand over Molly's. "Your bone structure, I think. And maybe around the mouth."

"Mich was very handsome. My mother said he looked like this famous Japanese movie star, Toshiro Mifune."

"Did your mother like him?" Molly asked.

"No. She has very mixed feelings about people from Japan. Sometimes I think it's a love-hate thing with her. She thinks a lot of them are arrogant and look down on Japanese who emigrated. As if all the Japanese-Canadians and - Americans were inferior creatures. She hates that attitude. But I think she has some pride in Japan, and she also hates the

271

Japan-bashing that happens when North Americans feel threatened economically."

"So she didn't approve of your relationship?" Ellie asked.

"Mich was an exchange student from Tokyo University. His family owns the Mori Corporation. It's not as large as Sony, but even back then it was becoming successful, and Mich was being groomed to be an executive. I was kind of a campus radical — I was into a lot of Asian political things, and I guess it fascinated him. He thought I was this wild and crazy artist."

"You're also very beautiful," Ellie smiled.

"Thank you." Karen seemed embarrassed. "Well, he told me he loved me, and I was in love with him — at least I thought I was. I don't know how much you know at eighteen." Karen smiled at Molly. "I didn't mean that the way it sounded.

"My mother said he was just using me. That his family would be disgraced if they knew he was involved with me. But I didn't believe her. I was sure he loved me."

"He was nineteen?" Ellie asked.

"Yes. I found out I was pregnant right before Mich was supposed to go back to Japan. I didn't know what I was going to do. When I told him, the first thing he said was that I would ruin his career and his life — and that because abortion wasn't legal in Canada, but was in Japan — he would arrange for an abortion for me there. But that I couldn't contact him when I went there to have it. That he could never see me again.

"My mother and my aunt made all the arrangements for me to go to the Evangeline Booth Home in Seattle, and she said if I kept the baby she would disown me. She had forbidden me to even say that I was of Japanese descent."

"So that's why we never knew," Ellie said quietly.

"She was so ashamed someone would find out. I was terrified — I did what she said." Karen took a tissue from her purse and blew her nose. "I'm sorry — I guess I didn't know this would be so hard." She took out another tissue and wiped her eyes. It was quiet for a few more minutes. "I never heard from him again."

"Does your mother know about us — that I found you?"

"Molly, she's ashamed. She still can't handle it."

"So she doesn't want to know much about me."

"I'm sorry, Molly," Karen said softly.

Molly looked at the picture in the yearbook. "I was hoping he was a good guy."

Ellie leaned close to her daughter. "You know who you are has nothing to do with what kind of person he is."

"I know, Mom." Molly looked across the table and her eyes met Karen's. "Your mother was awful about it — " She looked at Ellie and then at Karen. "I just want you to know how much I think it took for you to sign the consent form." Molly went around the

273

table and put her arms around Karen. As she hugged her, she whispered, "Karen — I'm so grateful you let me find you."

The three women talked late into the afternoon. Karen wanted Molly to be sure and send her a copy of the senior prom picture of her and Roland, Molly wanted a picture of Robbie with the Clayton Park Bluenosers, and Ellie wrote down the names of all the galleries in Vancouver that showed Karen's work, making a mental note to buy a painting for Molly for graduation.

After they had exhausted the soccer ball, the baseball and the Frisbee, Paul and Robbie headed back to the picnic table.

"Paul has a lot of pigs, Mom," Robbie said excitedly. "He dumps them in pressure chambers to find out about deep-sea diving and stuff, and he said that he was going to name the next one that was born Wayne Gretzky!"

The sun was beginning to set as they packed up the picnic things and all the photo albums.

"Thanks for the mud." Molly hugged Robbie.

"Thanks for the ash. Molly?"

"Yes?"

"I told my friend Timmy LeHavre about you, and I said I had a half sister, and he wanted to know why you weren't whole. You look like a whole person to me. Get it? Ha ha!"

"You look like a whole person to me, too, Robbie!"

Paul stood with his arm around his daughter and Robbie waited patiently while the two mothers hugged.

"How can I ever thank you enough?" Karen whispered.

"How can I ever thank you?" Ellie pressed her cheek against Karen's dark hair.

As they crossed the border and drove north into Canada, Robbie sat next to his mother, reaching into the plastic pouch and rubbing the volcanic ash between his fingers. "Mom?"

"What, Robbie?"

"Molly's nice."

"Yes, she is." Thank you, God, she said silently, for giving my baby such beautiful parents.

"Mom?"

"Hmmm?"

"Is Seattle near Disneyland?"

"Not exactly."

"I was thinking maybe I could go there with Molly someday."

"Maybe someday."

"I wish Dad could come with us."

"So do I." Karen looked over at him and patted his hand. "Maybe someday, Rob."

* * *

The Fletcher family decided to look at the Peace Arch before driving home. They walked through the park where it straddled the borders of the two countries and read the inscription on the Canadian side, *Brethren Dwelling Together in Unity*. Inside the arch was an open gate, and they each read the inscription; on the east wall was written *1814* and on the west wall, *May These Gates Never Be Closed*. They watched for a minute as Karen's car drove out of sight and then slowly the three of them crossed to the American side.

They stood together in front of it and looked up and read the top of the arch . . . *Children of a Common Mother*.

Molly reached for her mother's hand, and then her father's.

About the Author

Jean Davies Okimoto makes her Scholastic Hardcover debut with *Molly by Any Other Name*. Her other books include *My Mother Is Not Married to My Father*; *It's Just Too Much*; *Boomerang Kids: How To Live with Adult Children Who Return Home*; and the young adult novel *Jason's Women*. Ms. Okimoto lives in Seattle, Washington, where she is a volunteer writing tutor in the Seattle Author Mentor program and creator of the Mayor's Reading Awards for reading improvement in the Seattle public schools. She and her husband, Joe, have four grown children and two dogs, Harold and Maude.

point®

Other books you will enjoy, about real kids like you!